# Wander Canyon Courtship

## Allie Pleiter

HARLEQUIN® LOVE INSPIRED®

Recycling programs
for this product may
not exist in your area.

 LOVE INSPIRED BOOKS

ISBN-13: 978-1-335-42894-3

Wander Canyon Courtship

Copyright © 2019 by Alyse Stanko Pleiter

www.Harlequin.com

**Printed in U.S.A.**

**Allie Pleiter**, an award-winning author and RITA® Award finalist, writes both fiction and nonfiction. Her passion for knitting shows up in many of her books and all over her life. Entirely too fond of French macarons and lemon meringue pie, Allie spends her days writing books and avoiding housework. Allie grew up in Connecticut, holds a BS in speech from Northwestern University and lives near Chicago, Illinois.

Visit the Author Profile page
at Harlequin.com for more titles.

# He couldn't breathe properly with her staring at him like that...

"You okay?"

"Yeah, sure." Yvonne's voice was breathless.

A curl of panic gripped Chaz. "You need to be careful around livestock," he said in the most practical tone he could muster with the small tornado in his chest.

"Good to remember." Her awestruck tone took on a whole new timbre, which only added to his panic.

"So, that's the herd and the ranch." The absurd pronouncement made him want to whack his head.

"I see why you love it so much." She seemed as desperate to fill the air between them with words as he was. "It's beautiful."

It was as if every single detailed memory left a mark. "We should head back. Lunch will be ready and then we'll head into town."

"Sure," she said a bit too brightly as she settled herself into the passenger seat. "No problem at all."

That was where she was wrong.

Because Chaz didn't like the idea of Yvonne being anywhere in Wander Canyon—anywhere in Colorado for that matter—without him...and that was a very big problem indeed.

In memory of my dear father-in-law,
Les Pleiter,
who had his own wonderful whirlwind
senior romance.

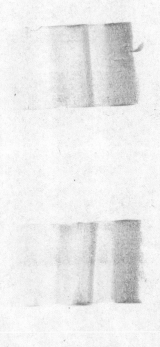

And he shall turn the heart of the fathers to the children, and the heart of the children to their fathers.

—*Malachi* 4:6

# Chapter One

Yvonne Niles gawked at the man standing at her bakery counter. "If I didn't know better, I'd think you don't want your dad to marry my aunt."

Chaz Walker ran one hand across his strong jawline. His glare told Yvonne that was *exactly* what he thought of Aunt Pauline's engagement to Hank Walker. "So I take it you're fine with it?" he challenged with intense, dark eyes.

Auntie P. and her beau, Hank, had been in her bakery shop not an hour ago choosing the cake for their upcoming Matrimony Valley wedding. The older couple seemed to be flat-out in love despite knowing each other for only a handful of months. Sure, the quickness of their engagement took everyone by surprise, but she wasn't about to confess her few niggling doubts to this man. "Not really my call, is it? Or yours."

She'd seen several control freaks as part of Matrimony Valley's now-thriving location wedding business, but this son's interference with his father's wedding topped the list. It was usually mothers of the bride who made life difficult. Son of the groom was a new one, to be sure.

"My dad just told me they ordered a chocolate wedding cake."

Yvonne put on her best bridezilla wrangler voice, which seemed ludicrous to use on the handsome yet brooding cowboy currently standing in her bakery. "Yes, Pauline wants me to make my signature Black Forest cake. Because she knows how good it is and how everybody loves it." It was true. That cake had been written up in *South-*

*eastern Nuptials* magazine as the best, most unusual wedding cake in the region. It was her signature cake. She pointed to the article and photograph framed on the bakery wall to underscore the point.

Were he not currently boasting a scowl cold enough to have frozen Matrimony Falls despite it being a very warm September, she might have called Chaz downright attractive. "My dad hates chocolate. She up and ordered a chocolate cake. Doesn't that tell you something?"

She'd met too many men like this—ones who could never understand why the rest of the world wouldn't bend to their will on even the tiniest of issues. Neal had been exactly like this. *Isn't that just the way?* she thought to herself. *The first good-looking single man to show up in the valley in a long time, and he turns out to be a self-centered know-it-all.* And about something as innocuous as his father's wedding cake, to boot.

Yvonne and her partners in the valley

didn't do cookie-cutter weddings. They created amazingly individualized nuptials. With a determined smile, Yvonne pulled out her sample book and paged over to a gorgeous *white*-iced Black Forest cake with luscious cherries and powdered-sugar-coated chocolate shavings piled on top. "Maybe your dad enjoys giving his bride a cake she likes. Couples do that, you know. At least the *happy* ones."

*Un*happy Chaz Walker glared at her for a moment, as if stunned by her refusal to see his side of things. Yvonne glared right back until the man silently turned on his boot heels and left the bakery.

She watched his long strides take him back across the street to where Chaz was staying with his father. Clearly he was strong, for when he reached the heavy front doors of Hailey's Inn Love, he yanked them open as easily as if they were paper. Auntie P. was about to become this grumpy cowboy's stepmother. Hadn't Mama always said, "You don't just marry a man, you marry his whole family"?

"Bless your heart, Auntie P.," Yvonne said aloud as she watched the door shut behind the broad-shouldered man. "I think you've got one rough ride ahead."

Yvonne sat down next to her aunt half an hour later as the high noon sun cast glorious colors on the Smoky Mountains behind Matrimony Falls. "Auntie P., I need to talk to you about something."

The clearing where they sat looked as beautiful as an oil painting. Almost two dozen happy brides and grooms had been united in the open-air "cathedral" that had been built in this grove. The grand and peaceful spot was among her very favorite places on earth—and perhaps the best place to have what might be a tough conversation.

Pauline gave her a concerned look. "What's wrong?"

Yvonne had rehearsed six different ways

to bring the subject up, but she opted to ditch them all in favor of a direct approach. "How do you think Chaz feels about your wedding?"

Pauline surprised her by frowning. "Oh, he's not especially in favor of it."

Yvonne fought the urge to pick her jaw up off the grass. "You knew?"

"Well, of course I know. The man's about as transparent as glass—not that he goes to much effort to hide his concerns."

"Doesn't that bother you?"

Pauline raised a dubious eyebrow. "Have you spent even ten minutes with Chaz?"

"He came into the bakery a bit ago." She might have found his eyes stunning were they not framed in a face that seemed to be stuck in a perpetual scowl. As it was, Chaz bore little resemblance to the happy, love-struck groom who had told Pauline to "order whatever cake her heart desires." Like father, like son? Hardly. "He gave me an earful about your wedding cake."

"Our cake? Oh, the chocolate part, I'm sure. He and Hank are die-hard vanilla fans. It's why I chose the white icing, but I expect he didn't give you a chance to explain that." Pauline folded her hands in her lap. "I'm sure you realized Chaz doesn't have a high opinion of anything. I don't take his doubts personally." She gave a small laugh. "Shame to waste those fine features on such a sourpuss, don't you think? Some days I think he hates everything and everybody."

Yvonne couldn't believe Pauline's laugh. "So you're okay with this?"

Pauline fluttered one hand. "Well, of course not. Why do you think he's here? It's not as if I need his help to organize a wedding. That's what y'all do here, isn't it?"

Not just Yvonne's, but the jobs of most people in the valley now centered on creating weddings. Mayor Jean Matrim Tyler— who herself was married in front of these falls just last winter—had cast a vision to reinvent this dying mill town into a destination wedding location. That dream had started to really take hold, and several brides—another of Yvonne's dear friends, the town florist, Kelly, among them—had followed suit earlier this year. In fact, the prime wedding season just wrapping up had been the most successful to date.

None of which could explain the restlessness in Yvonne's soul. Even the chance to give Pauline the wedding of her dreams hadn't drowned out the hum of dissatisfaction. "I don't think bringing him here helped convince him to get on board." Aunt Pauline was never one to back down from a challenge, but Yvonne thought she might have chosen a monster of an obstacle in trying to gain Chaz's endorsement.

"What is it you always say?" Pauline asked. "Folks argue about cake and flowers when they can't bring themselves to argue about the real stuff? Chaz thinks we're moving way too fast."

Yvonne had to give her aunt credit. Most

brides she knew would take serious offense at that, but Pauline seemed to accept it without bile.

"Of course, it's not really me he's wary of. It's change. He can't stomach that his daddy—we all know Hank is Chaz's step-daddy but that doesn't change anything—is moving on and making choices Chaz doesn't agree with."

As a matter of fact, she didn't know Chaz was Hank's stepson. He referred to Hank as "Dad" in the bakery. She'd called Hank "your dad" right in front of Chaz and he'd not corrected her. Pauline had told her Hank was a widower with two sons. Yvonne had assumed Chaz and his brother were from that earlier marriage. Evidently not. "Hank's been married *twice* before?" It would have been nicer not to sound so shocked.

"Wyatt is from Hank's first marriage when he was very young. Wyatt's mama left Hank when Wyatt was still a little thing." She gave a sigh. "I think that's why Wyatt is such a mess. Little boys don't get over things like that, even though they'd never admit that. Mariah—who'd had a terrible marriage of her own—came along with Chaz in tow about seven years later. They had loads of happy years together before Mariah died. So only Wyatt is Hank's blood son. He treats both boys well, but I think they still feel the difference. Those two men couldn't *be* more different."

"How so?"

"Well, you've met Chaz. A handsome fella, but a bit of a stick-in-the-mud. Sure he knows how everything ought to be."

She'd had only one conversation with the man, but handsome know-it-all seemed a fair assessment of Chaz. "And Wyatt?"

"The opposite of all that. A lost soul. Bit of a black sheep who's never rebelled far enough to actually leave home. Can't quite get his ducks in a row and isn't even sure he wants to." Pauline looked at Yvonne. "In other words, everything Chaz isn't…including blood."

"And you want to marry into this mess of a family?" Yvonne winced. When was she going to learn to think before blurting things like that out?

Pauline got that dreamy look in her eye Yvonne saw on every Matrimony Valley bride. "I'd marry into ten messes for Hank. I've waited a long time to lose my heart, honey. I'm not about to let a whopping case of sibling rivalry scare me off my chance."

"I don't think there's anything that scares you, Auntie P."

"Oh, I don't know about that. But I don't expect you young people to understand how easy it is to be certain of what you want at our age." Her aunt's choice of words sent a pang of guilt between Yvonne's ribs. After all, she'd had her own doubts about the speedy engagement and not had the nerve to say anything that might dampen Auntie P.'s happiness.

"So you're sure about Hank?" was the most she could muster.

"No one's ever sure, darlin'. But waiting for sure doesn't make much sense when you've only got so many years left on this earth."

Yvonne never liked it when Pauline talked like that. Pauline was younger in her seventies than most people in their fifties. "Oh, Auntie P., you'll live forever."

Pauline put her arm around Yvonne and gave her a big hug. Pauline gave the best hugs—no holding back, never the first to let go. So different from Mama's careful embraces. "I will in heaven, baby. That's where eternity happens. But here on earth, the clock's a tickin'." She plopped a big kiss on the top of Yvonne's head, just the way she'd done since Yvonne was a little girl. "Hank says he has a big announcement to make at dinner tonight. Let's just say a big prayer that whatever it is will smooth things over a bit."

A big prayer indeed. Yvonne put her head on Pauline's shoulder. *When I grow up, I want to be just like her. Faith-filled and feisty and fearless.*

## Chapter Two

When Chaz opened the hotel room door after lunch, he expected to see Dad in hip waders, ready to spend the afternoon fly-fishing. Instead, the man wore khakis and a bright green polo shirt. A polo shirt was something he'd never seen Dad in before. Were it not for the familiar boots under the khakis, Chaz might have had to look twice to see if it really was Dad.

"Change of plans," Dad said, stating the obvious with an apologetic smile. "So you're gonna want to change your clothes."

Chaz had been looking forward to a few hours of peaceful fly-fishing. This morning's ridiculous standoff with the pretty-but-annoying baker had put him in an irritated mood, and he was looking forward to some quiet companionship. The sport was one of the things he enjoyed most with his father—it always fed both their spirits. And since Wyatt had never possessed the patience required of a fisherman, it had been something unique to the relationship between Chaz and his dad.

Something he clearly wasn't going to get to do today.

"I'm not dressing like that," he said, trying—but not necessarily succeeding—to keep his voice light and teasing as he motioned Dad into the room.

Hank puffed up his chest at his uncharacteristic attire. "Pauline bought these for me."

*I could have guessed that*, Chaz thought sourly as he closed the door. He opted instead to strive for a reluctant compliment. "Very spiffy." Leery of the new agenda for the afternoon, he asked, "So we're going someplace else instead of fishing?"

"Okay by you?" Dad asked.

The earnest look on Dad's face made it impossible for Chaz to say anything but "Sure. As long as I don't have to put on a tie or anything."

"I should check, but I don't think so."

*You don't think so?* Chaz swallowed his annoyance. He hadn't packed a tie. Dad hated ties. Why should he even need to check if they were doing something requiring a tie?

Then again, Chaz hadn't expected to be here at all. There seemed to be no logical reason why Dad invited him on this wedding planning trip. Dad had to know he wasn't thrilled at the prospect of leaving the ranch in Wyatt's care. Wyatt could barely run the ranch for an hour on his own. Chaz couldn't fathom how he'd handle the five days they were here in Matrimony Valley to firm up wedding plans and for Hank and

Pauline to attend a wedding of a friend of Pauline's. *It's pointless for me to be here. Why did I ever let Dad talk me into coming?*

"Pauline is taking all of us to the Biltmore this afternoon," Dad pronounced. "It's a big fancy estate over by Asheville. Wedding's mostly nailed down, so we can do a bit of sightseeing before that nice steak dinner I promised you."

Chaz picked those three sentences apart. "Wedding's mostly nailed down" meant that choices had already been made, and his mission to salvage at least some of this event for his dad with any degree of male dignity was probably all but gone. "Big fancy estate" sounded like nothing he'd find interesting or a remotely fair trade-off for time spent fishing with his father. Most worrisome of all, "All of us" meant that not only was he expected to go on this fussy field trip, but it was also likely Yvonne would be coming, as well.

"You want to go visit some fancy house?"

Chaz asked, swallowing back "instead of going fishing?"

"Pauline's all excited about it." Dad scratched his chin as if, like Chaz, he wasn't quite sure what the allure of walking all around someone else's property was. "I'm gonna need you along so I don't drown in girl talk."

So Yvonne *was* going. He still didn't know what to make of that woman. His mind kept replaying their conversation. His brain kept bringing up the picture of her eyeing him like she had him all figured out—bright eyes blazing, chin raised in defiance, hands planted on curvy hips. Under other circumstances, he might have found her amusing, even attractive. But here, she was just another of the army of people who seemed to be trying to marry Dad off as fast as possible.

A rebellious part of him hoped Wyatt would do what Wyatt always did—end up knee-deep in some sort of ranch problem.

Maybe he could play that into necessitating the next flight to Colorado.

His sense of loyalty won out, however, and he managed a flat-sounding "No problem."

Dad forced a grin. "I want you to spend time with Pauline. Get to know her better."

Dad was trying so hard to make this work. While Chaz had tried to hide his resistance to this new relationship, Dad's forced grin told him he hadn't quite succeeded. Dad wanted him to bubble over with enthusiasm, to look at this whirlwind courtship as an exhilarating launch. They'd met online, for crying out loud. Even if it was a Christian seniors dating site, could anything like that really be trusted? To Chaz the whole thing smacked of a leap off a dangerously high cliff. "Give me a few minutes to change."

Ten minutes later, he found himself walking down Aisle Avenue with Dad. As he passed all the wedding-named shops—the Love in Bloom Flower Shop, the Sweet

Hearts Ice Cream Parlor and even the Catch Your Match fishing outfitters he'd optimistically stopped in to purchase a few new flies that now would get no use—Chaz felt his spirits fall. The whole idea of this wedding had bothered him from the first, and Dad's obvious hope that coming here would curb his resistance was a losing proposition.

As if their unappealing destination wasn't bad enough, a white van with the words *Bliss Bakery* painted on the side in swirly letters sat parked in front of the bakery. Yvonne and Pauline stood waiting beside it.

"Yvonne decided this'd be the best car to take all of us," Hank explained at Chaz's gape of surprise.

"No kidding," Chaz said, unable to come up with a better response.

"It's one of those convertible numbers where the rear seats and cargo bay can be switched around," Hank pressed.

As it turned out, the vehicle was surprisingly comfortable—if you didn't pay attention to how Hank and Pauline snuggled in the back seat as if he and Yvonne were dropping them off at the junior prom.

The mountain roads made for tricky driving, and more than once Chaz fought the urge to grab tighter hold of his armrest. Even under good circumstances, he was a terrible passenger, always preferring being behind the wheel. More than once Yvonne gave him a look when he tensed up over how she took a turn or checked the mirror before she changed lanes. *Cut me some slack. I'm way out of my depth here*, he wanted to yell, but clamped his mouth shut.

Forty tense minutes later, he, Dad, Pauline and Yvonne got out of the van to stare at the biggest house Chaz had ever seen. *Mansion* really was the right word for the place. It was practically a castle, with monstrous manicured lawns and acres of formal gardens.

And the rooms. Of course they had to tour the rooms. It seemed as if they went on forever, each one fancier than the last. He counted twenty-four chairs at the dining room table just off a fireplace that looked big enough to roast an entire steer. The oohs and aahs around him told Chaz some people clearly thought the tour was fascinating. He just wasn't one of them.

"The estate does over two hundred weddings a year," Yvonne offered as they walked through yet another ballroom-looking space. She kept rubbing one eye as if it were bothering her. "I'd consider myself hitting the big time if I got to do even one of them."

"Could you do it?" he wondered aloud. "Do a cake for something as big as this place holds?" The sheer size of any party held here probably needed a whole team of bakers.

She sighed. "Not yet. But I'd sure like to. Be a swanky, respected vendor able to pull off a venue like this? It's definitely a goal."

She fussed with her eye again, blinking

and rubbing it so much that he felt compelled to ask, "Are you okay?"

She looked at him as if such a kindness were out of character for him. "It's just my contact lens. It's been bugging me the whole day." She squinted at him with her one good eye. "I'll be fine." Wyatt may lay claim to being the ladies' man of the family, but even Chaz had been around enough women in his life to know when the word *fine*—especially when said in that tone—meant anything but.

She'd been making conversation—or trying to—the whole afternoon. *Be nice*, he told himself. He did admire her ambition, and she was clearly talented. Normally he liked direct people—when he wasn't in complete disagreement with them, that was. "If you want to be a swanky, respectable baker, why hide out in Matrimony Valley? Wouldn't it be better to have your shop down in Asheville, where the swanky, respectable brides are?"

"Do you try hard?" One hand planted itself on her hip again. "Or does being such a curmudgeon just come to you naturally?"

He laughed at her choice of words—he liked that Yvonne gave as good as she got. But she hadn't answered his question, and that told him something.

Rather than press his luck, Chaz directed his attention over to Dad and Pauline. The couple stood gazing dreamily out over a nearby balcony. A harrowing thought came to him, and he turned back to Yvonne. "Those two didn't think about getting hitched here, did they?"

Now it was Yvonne's turn to laugh—a musical, full-hearted sound he found himself enjoying a bit too much. "You don't get hitched at the Biltmore," she replied. "And no, even if they could afford it—which no one I know can—it isn't really their style, wouldn't you say?"

She gave him another lopsided look—squinting with one eye, glaring with the other—as she tucked her hair behind one ear. The shoulder-length honey-blond locks that had been up in a ponytail in the bakery were down now, held back with a bright blue headband. September could still be surprisingly warm in this part of the country, so she and Pauline were both in brightly colored dresses. Pauline's was some sort of purple pattern while Yvonne's was a pale yellow that lit up her skin and made the blue of her eyes stand out. Not that he noticed. It was mostly that he felt out of place in his black jeans, white shirt and boots. Stark and practical beside the breezy colors the rest of them wore. Dad? In khakis? It was as if they'd gotten off the airplane in another universe.

"Look at them," Yvonne said, nodding toward their respective relatives. "They're like teenagers."

He scoffed. "No offense, but my experience of teenagers is that they let their urges overpower their brains and make choices everybody regrets later."

Even the squinted blue eye flashed fire at that. "They're grown-ups, Chaz."

It was the first time she'd said his name. She drew the *z* out, her hint of a Southern accent giving it a swingy quality. She was on the opposing team here, and liking her—even a little—only made things more complicated, right?

He decided it was time to dive right into it. "You're really okay with this? With them?"

She hesitated just a second before replying. "Of course. But it's pretty clear you aren't."

Dad was holding Pauline's hand, leaning close to her and saying things that made her laugh. No, giggle. It was both amusing and a little bit sickening. Shades of Wyatt turning on the million-watt charm. Had he ever in his life—even as a teen—been that smitten?

Chaz stepped back and scratched his

chin. He focused on facts. "It's been awfully fast."

"Some might say that."

A tiny crack in the wall of support she'd been showing. "And you're a hundred percent okay with how fast?"

"It doesn't matter what percent okay I am with it. Hank and Pauline have every right to get married as fast or as slow as they like."

That was another crack, as far as he was concerned. He turned to face her squarely. "I wasn't asking if they had a right—of course they have the right. I was asking what you think of it."

They locked gazes for a long moment. He didn't look away or back down because he knew she was deciding how honest to be.

"I think it's brave."

Brave, huh? That answer told him a lot.

The good news was that even the worst day could be salvaged by a very good steak, and the meal in front of Chaz was excellent. Dad had said a heartwarming grace over the food, thanking God for his new family.

The prayer woke Chaz up to the unsettling notion that soon he would be related to the woman whom he'd just spent the afternoon with matching wits.

"I've been reading up on how they handed down the estate a few years back," Dad said as they talked about the grandeur of the Biltmore property. "Pretty amazing how a place that large is still privately owned."

It made sense that Dad would notice that. The succession plans for large establishments like their own Wander Canyon Ranch in states like Colorado and Wyoming were a huge issue. Chaz himself had been trying to broach it with Dad for the past two years. "Who owns it now?"

"The owner who came back and turned it into the tourist attraction it is now left it to his son," Yvonne offered.

"Smart move to keep it in the family," Dad said. Chaz was inclined to agree, but something in his gut noticed his father's tone wasn't entirely casual.

"I think it's always the best thing to do," Pauline said. "Yvonne lives in the house my sister and I grew up in, and I love that it's stayed in the family. Everything is so transient now. Family homes hardly ever happen anymore, don't you think?"

"Where's your mom now?" Chaz asked Yvonne.

"She lives in Charlotte, where my two sisters have settled." Yvonne reached for the bread basket, and he watched her inspect the rolls with a baker's professional eye before selecting one. "Janice and Rita run a super successful chain of boutiques there."

She said *super successful* with just enough of an edge to let Chaz know there was some tension there.

Pauline jumped in. "Have we told you where we're going on our honeymoon?"

she asked in a bright, let's-change-the-subject tone. "We're going to Paris for a whole month."

"Paris, *France*?" Chaz couldn't hide his surprise. Dad didn't travel—*before*. Dad was easily, willingly turning himself inside out to please Pauline. Was that really how love worked, turning sensible men into complete fools? Mom claimed to love Hank with all her heart when she was alive, but she'd never transformed into someone he didn't recognize like Hank was doing lately. Dad was becoming a complete stranger, and that lit a slow spark of panic deep in Chaz's gut. "For a month? That's a really long time to be away from the ranch."

Hank drew in a big breath. "Been giving that a lot of thought, actually. I've been thinking it might be getting close to my time to retire. Hand the ranch on down."

*Is that why I'm here?* Maybe Dad wanted to work it out together before bringing back a plan to Wyatt.

Dad cleared his throat. "Course, they say it's always best if the acreage stays intact. You don't want to split it up if you can help it. My granddaddy bought that land," Dad started explaining to Pauline. "My father worked it after him. It's the Walker legacy, that land is." He turned back to Chaz. "It's time that Wyatt and you stepped into those boots. Without me, that is. And my honeymoon is a good time to get that started."

Dad had listed Wyatt first, putting an unnatural emphasis on Wyatt's name. Chaz's pulse froze for a moment. Dad had just said the ranch would stay undivided. The hairs on the back of Chaz's neck prickled. Blood was about to win out. Over the thing he cared about most in the world.

# Chapter Three

It was as if a bomb had just been dropped in the room. Yvonne didn't fully understand what was being said, only that it was large and unexpected and volatile.

In the chair next to her, Chaz was practically rattling with cold, barely held-in-check alarm. He stared straight at his stepfather and said very slowly, "What are you saying?"

The tone sent a chill down her back. Pauline set down her fork and gave Yvonne a *brace yourself* look.

Hank straightened as he met Chaz's glower. "I'm saying I want you to manage

Wander Canyon Ranch while I'm gone and when I retire."

"Manage," Chaz repeated.

"That's what I said."

"Manage isn't own." Chaz's voice somehow managed to get lower and colder.

Hank didn't flinch. "No, it's not."

Yvonne had the vision of two enormous bulls stomping and snorting at each other, each waiting for the other to charge. She busied herself with the irritable contact lens, needing something to do rather than watch this unfold. Why had Hank done this in front of her and Pauline? This should have been a private conversation between Chaz and his stepfather.

She realized, at that moment, what was actually happening. A surge of compassion rose up in her chest for Chaz. What a blindsiding blow to receive in front of strangers.

Hank cleared his throat. "The land is best kept in one piece, son. You know that."

It seemed a cruel detail that Hank chose

to use the word *son* at this moment. Chaz tightened his grip on the steak knife he was still holding, his knuckles white and his forearms flexing.

"A choice had to be made," Hank continued. "One we all knew was coming someday, so I chose to make it now. We all want it to stay Walker land, don't we?"

"*My* last name is Walker," Chaz practically ground out through his teeth. "I have never, ever regretted changing my last name. Until now."

Chaz put the knife down on the table in something just short of a slam. "Seems I've never been anything more than a stepson after all."

"Chaz," Pauline began, scrambling for calm Yvonne saw no signs of coming.

"Don't!" Chaz shot back, scowling at her as if she'd put Hank up to this. "Don't you even—"

"Don't you talk like that to my bride,"

Hank growled back with a force equal to Chaz's tone. "I get you may be upset."

"*May* be?" Chaz shouted. People around the restaurant began to stare. Yvonne and Pauline traded cautious looks, wondering what to do if one of the men would stalk from the room or throw a punch.

Yvonne sent a prayer flying up that Chaz and Hank would remember they were in public and miles from home. It seemed that Chaz somehow overheard her prayer, for he lowered his voice, but still jabbed a finger at her and Pauline.

"Is that why you did this here? In front of them? So I wouldn't haul off at you like I want to right now? Manage Wander Canyon? *Manage?* No wonder you bailed on fishing. You know what I would have done had we been alone. Well played, Dad." Chaz spit the final word out with such bitterness Yvonne felt it stab her chest. "You always did know how to drop a bomb."

Yvonne looked to Hank's reaction. He

looked pained, but not ashamed, or regretful, or in any way unsure of his decision.

Auntie P. wasn't marrying into a tangle. She was marrying into an all-out war.

Yvonne could barely believe they didn't leave right there and then, but it was as if neither Chaz nor Hank would flinch first. Eat? Now? She was practically nauseous from the anger flowing between those two men.

She'd never been so grateful to lose a contact lens in her life. She didn't even bother to really look for it, just pounced on it as a reason to wrap up this torturous meal and go home. There wasn't a dessert in the world worth staying at this table for.

"I'll drive," Chaz declared as they reached the parking lot, grabbing the keys out of her hand when she pulled them from her bag. At least it would give him something to do—he'd probably implode from just having to sit steaming in the passenger seat.

Only that left *her* in that passenger seat as she directed Chaz home along the back roads toward Matrimony Valley. The van echoed with an icy silence, Hank and Pauline huddling in the back seat holding hands and exchanging wary looks. Chaz gripped the steering wheel and drove with careful, angry precision.

And silence. He merely nodded at her directions to turn here or there, barely uttering a word since they left the table. Even with half her vision blurred, Chaz looked angry enough to walk the forty-some miles back to the valley.

*Now what?* Yvonne's brain spun in a dozen directions trying to figure out what to do next. Short of enduring the drive in ragged silence, there seemed to be nothing to say or do. There was no way to make this less awkward. There simply was…

A dark mound loomed into her headlights without warning. "Look out!" she cried and Chaz stomped on the brakes, but not before a heartrending thud and bump announced they'd hit whatever it was. Chaz wrestled for control of the van as it screeched into a slow-motion, tilting arc that veered it off the road.

Yvonne yelped as she was knocked against the van door, and Pauline and Hank gasped as they were tossed about in the back seat. The airbags deployed and deflated in a heartbeat, leaving Yvonne stunned by the sudden whack back against her headrest. For a moment she couldn't breathe.

"What…?" Hank gasped, coughing. Yvonne tried to pull in a breath to answer and found her lungs didn't work. She tried to ascertain what had just happened, but all she could take in was a hissing, ticking sound and the smoke rising off the crunched front of her van. *No. Oh, no. Please no.* Absurdly, her brain reminded her she had only four payments to go on the vehicle.

"Is anyone hurt?" It was the first words Chaz had spoken in half an hour. He was shaking his head, recovering from the whack of the driver's-side airbag now hanging deflated from the center of the steering wheel.

"I…don't think so." Yvonne gulped, finally able to breathe. Her shoulder felt pummeled by the seat belt, her cheeks stung from the slap of the airbag, but she hadn't hit her head, and her arms and legs seemed to move freely.

"Dad?" The raw panic in Chaz's voice pricked Yvonne's heart—such a different tone from what he'd used at the table. Anger hadn't erased every bit of love and worry, just most of it, and hopefully only for now.

"Auntie P.?" she said, twisting around to see Hank and her aunt righting themselves from where they'd tumbled over in the crash.

"We're okay back here," Pauline said in a breathless gasp. Yvonne saw no blood or evidence of any injury.

Chaz looked at her, his features sharp in the moonlight. "Are you okay?"

"I think so," she replied, even though she didn't feel anything close to okay.

"What was that in the road?" Hank asked.

Yvonne looked up the embankment to see the silhouette of an animal struggling in the road. Based on the whining sounds, it was injured. Could tonight get any worse?

"That sounds like a dog," Pauline said, worry pitching her voice high.

"Or a fox or a wolf," Hank cautioned.

Chaz took immediate control of the situation, holding out his hand. "Give me your phone to call 911. Your local number will be better to call from than mine." Rather than be annoyed, Yvonne found herself grateful. One hour's curmudgeon was another hour's useful hero, it seemed.

Yvonne undid her seat belt and began hunting on the car floor where her handbag had spilled its contents. She unlocked the cell phone and handed it to him.

"Where are we?"

It took a minute for her fog to lift enough to name the back road she'd chosen instead of the highway.

He peered through the window, which thankfully hadn't been broken in the impact. Yvonne said a prayer of thanks that they hadn't been in Pauline's small sedan or hit one of the many elk that populated the area. "Okay." The animal's cries pitched higher. "I'll go look for a mile marker up there. Got a flashlight?"

"Just the one on my cell phone," she admitted.

With a glare, Chaz pushed the groaning driver's-side door open to reveal a wall of leaves. Without hesitation, he stepped out into the thick foliage and began clambering toward the road and whatever lay injured on it.

Yvonne knew this road well, but the dark of the night and the lack of any other cars on the road made it seem like the middle of nowhere.

"What did we hit?" Pauline asked.

"That animal up there and the tree in front of us." Yvonne's door practically fell open from the sharp incline of the van's resting angle. One headlight sputtered and failed as if to announce the vehicle's demise. *Totaled,* her mind assessed, though she couldn't even see all the damage. "Are you two hurt at all?"

"No," Pauline said. "A bump or bruise I'll feel tomorrow maybe, but nothing more than that. Hank, honey?"

"Fine. And praise God, glad to be so. That was close," he answered. He began to undo the seat belts and maneuver himself and Pauline up to get out of the car.

"Okay, then." Yvonne stepped out of the car and climbed the short rise to where Chaz was crouched over the animal. She walked closer to see him talking to what looked like a German shepherd mix dog gasping in short, shallow pants.

Chaz pulled his belt from his jeans and looked back at her over his shoulder. "Find me two branches. Long and straight as you can manage."

"Is he okay?" she asked, noting the dog's unnaturally bent leg.

"No. But I think we only broke his leg. Branches," he repeated. "Fast." He turned back to the animal, stroking its head as the dog looked about with wild eyes. His voice held a caretaker's calm assurance. "Easy there, big fella. We'll get you out of this mess."

Looking for branches in the middle of the night with only one contact lens seemed a rather daunting task, but Yvonne began to look around. "Chaz, be careful."

"Bit late for that." Despite the cool of the evening, Chaz pulled off his shirt and then the T-shirt underneath. Somehow he managed to look even larger than his already considerable height. Muscular, lean and strong. The dog gave a desperate whine as he wrapped the T-shirt around the bleeding leg. "I know it hurts. Just hang in there."

She managed to find two decent-sized sticks in short order, delivering them to Chaz. He'd pulled his shirt back on but otherwise stayed focused on the animal, talking in low and steady tones. With the practiced hands of someone who tended to animals, he lined the sticks up on either side of the wrapped injured leg and secured it with his belt.

"You watch yourself there. You never know what an injured animal will do," Hank warned as he and Pauline came up from the van.

"It's a dog, Dad, not a bear. No collar, but it could be chipped." With an eerie feeling, Yvonne noticed he had placed himself between the animal and her, Hank and Pauline.

Chaz's calm control set all of them at

ease. The dog tried to get up, but Chaz gently held it still. Yvonne watched regret and compassion battle in Chaz's eyes. The accident showed her a different side of this man, one that tugged at her in ways that made little sense. There was more to Chaz Walker than just Pauline's sourpuss label.

By the time the thin, high wail of a siren finally cut through the silence, Yvonne could honestly say she was grateful Chaz was nearby.

## *Chapter Four*

Chaz let out a breath of relief as he listened to the emergency veterinarian's report. "Broken leg, skin lesions, but nothing that can't heal in time."

"Can you contact the owner?" Yvonne asked. She looked beyond tired, and Chaz supposed that for a woman who normally kept the early morning hours of a bakery, 11:30 p.m. felt like the middle of the night. He'd found it a kindness that she'd stayed with him, even though Dad and Pauline had already gone back with the tow truck that had taken what was left of Yvonne's van back home. He was pretty sure it was totaled, and she seemed to agree, but neither of them spoke of it.

"It'd be the first thing I'd do, if I knew who the owner was," the vet replied. "This guy's got no microchip, and if he had a collar it's long gone. The best we can do is provide a description to the sheriff and keep him here."

Chaz took one look at the bank of crates in the room behind them and felt his stomach tighten. "I'll cover the bills," he offered, "but then what happens?" This dog's desperate eyes had hooked into him back there on the roadside and hadn't let go since. He'd run a ranch for years. He was no stranger to the injury and even the death of animals. He couldn't explain why this was different but it was.

The vet shrugged her shoulders. "Shelter, most likely."

That wasn't the answer he wanted to hear. "And then what?"

The vet gave a *do you really want me*

*to say it?* look that made Chaz want to punch something.

His response was instantaneous. "So he comes back with us."

That declaration woke Yvonne right up. "To the valley?"

"Do you have a vet in town?" the doctor asked, her eyebrow raised.

Yvonne pushed her hair back from her face. "Dan Mullins, but…"

Chaz cut in, eyes steady on the vet. "Can the dog safely travel to…" The town's name still felt silly on his tongue. "…Matrimony Valley?"

The doctor's gaze flicked to Yvonne as if they might be able to talk him out of this. Not a chance. Chaz had made up his mind. He'd wounded this dog. He wasn't going to leave him to whimper in some cage. He wouldn't let this dog be abandoned by whatever idiot had left him wandering a mountain roadside at night.

"The leg's cast. He's in stable condition,"

the vet replied. "It's just painkillers, antibiotics, rest and regular meals from here. I can send the X-rays with you. Honestly, he's likely to try walking in a few hours. If he can manage the cast, short walks outside for necessary business should be okay."

"Then he comes with us."

Yvonne rubbed her eyes. "Bruce Lohan's coming with his truck to pick us up. I suppose there's room…"

"He'll ride on my lap if he has to." The practicalities of what he would do with the dog when he got back to the valley didn't matter. He wasn't going to have the final act of this terrible day be him abandoning a dog. Especially not one he'd injured.

He'd never had a dog of his own because Wyatt's dog, Rocker, was just plain mean to other dogs. He'd meant to get one of his own when Dad had given him the guesthouse on the ranch, but never got around to it.

Before tonight, he'd thought of that guesthouse as a sign of independence, of Dad recognizing the need for his own space. Now it just felt like a demotion, as if he'd been put out of the big house where Dad and Wyatt lived. The way you put a dog out in a doghouse.

The dog was going to be his, period.

Yvonne had the good sense to recognize this was not open for discussion. "Okay, then," she said cautiously as she pulled out her phone. "I'll send a text to Bruce that he's got another passenger."

"Good."

"But the inn." Yvonne pursed her lips. "Hailey doesn't have rooms that allow pets."

The idea that this dog might give him a way out of that fussy inn made him that much more indebted to the beast. The last thing he wanted right now was to be under the same roof with his stepfather. "So we do something else."

Yvonne's face brightened. "Bruce and Kelly have a cabin they rent in the back of their property. You might be able to stay there." She raised her phone and stepped from the exam room. "I'll go check."

"Looks like you just got yourself a dog." The vet clicked her pen and picked up a clipboard. "Name?"

"Charles Walker."

She smiled. "We covered that already. I meant the dog's name."

Chaz rubbed his eyes. He was weary on so many levels it felt like his soul ached. "I have to name the dog right now?"

"Well, no, but…"

Without warning, Chaz's mind brought up the story of William Cecil, the son who'd returned to the Biltmore estate when it was in bad straits. The son who'd fought to turn the failing property into the massive enterprise he'd spent the afternoon wandering.

It seemed as good a name as any. "Cecil."

After a questioning look, the vet filled in her chart. "Cecil it is. I'll give you a week's supply of medicine to control pain and infection. I'll throw in a blanket to take him home in, too. I'll send word to this Dr. Mullins in Matrimony Valley to see Cecil tomorrow for follow-up. We've done the rabies, but Mullins can get him brought up to date on his other shots. I'll go get that blanket, and a meal or two's worth of food to tide you over." With that, the vet left the room.

Cecil, somehow sensing the weight of the moment, looked up at Chaz with worried eyes. The frightened plea in those eyes sealed it. As of this moment, Chaz would have walked all the way back to the valley carrying the animal rather than leave him here.

"Cecil okay for a name?" he asked, feeling foolish.

Cecil licked his palm and settled his head against Chaz's hand, closing his eyes in rest. It must have been sheer exhaustion that choked his throat at that moment, not any loyalty to this scruffy canine or the weight of obligation he felt looking at the freshly applied cast.

It didn't matter that it made no sense, and he had no idea what was going to happen after tomorrow morning. How the dog was going to get back to Wander Canyon didn't matter. Whether or not Chaz even had a Wander Canyon Ranch to go back to after this whole wedding mess was a problem for another day. This was one thing he could set right in a whole heap of "not right" all around him today.

Yvonne stepped back into the room, yawning. "Bruce will be here in twenty minutes, and you can stay in the cabin for the rest of your visit."

"Cecil and I appreciate it."

She gaped at him. "Cecil?"

"Cecil," he replied, simply nodding. Even if he had an explanation for how and why he'd just named the dog—which he didn't—he couldn't put it into words anyhow.

She gave him an understanding smile.

Her soft eyes told him Yvonne recognized why Cecil couldn't go anywhere but home with him. "Hello, Cecil," she said, touching the dog's dark, velvety ear. Cecil gave a low moan that sounded far too much like a contented sigh.

As for Chaz, the warmth in Yvonne's voice settled into his chest before he could stop it.

Most mornings Yvonne loved the solitude of the bakery. There was a glorious optimism in creating delicious things before most of the world had even opened their eyes.

Not today.

With an out-of-commission van and a sleep-deprived brain, the ovens seemed more like taskmasters than partners this morning. Dawn came blaring through the windows, and there didn't seem to be enough coffee in North Carolina, much less in her corner of Matrimony Valley.

Not too long after the school bus rumbled down the street, Yvonne looked up from a tray of cinnamon rolls to see Kelly Lohan, Bruce's wife and the town florist, coming through the doors.

"I was sure I'd find Cathy Bolton behind the counter this morning. You can't have gotten much sleep last night."

"She's coming in later to hold down the fort when I go over to Ziggy's." Jerome Zigler of Ziggy's Valley Garage had towed the van all the way back to Matrimony Valley last night, but gave no indication of a prognosis. Yvonne offered her friend an apologetic grimace. "Sorry to haul Bruce out in the middle of the night."

"It wasn't the first time. And it was for you." Bruce was now a helicopter pilot for a commercial firm, but he had been a Forest Service pilot when he'd first come to the valley. The tale of how Bruce and Kelly fell for each other during one of the valley's most calamitous snowbound weddings was one that had warmed everyone's heart.

"Well," Kelly continued, "you and Chaz Walker and now an adorable dog named… Cecil?"

"Yeah, I'm still not quite sure how that happened. But I have to admit, it's sweet and rather noble. Chaz Walker is certainly a load of surprises—good and bad." Yvonne slid a tray of sugary spirals into the waiting oven. "You're okay with putting them up?"

"The cabin was empty. Better our cabin than asking Hailey to break policy, and you should have seen how Lulu and Carly went crazy over the dog this morning. I had to practically push them onto the school bus. Someone ought to warn poor Cecil he'll be getting loads of little-girl care while he heals."

Kelly's daughter, Lulu, had connected strongly with Bruce's daughter, Carly, when they had visited for the wedding, and the two girls had contrived mightily to get their parents together so they could become sisters. Their new family was one of Yvonne's favorite Matrimony Valley happy endings.

Little girls smothering Cecil meant little girls around Chaz. She had to admit, it might be amusing to watch that man handle such a heavy dose of cuteness.

Kelly leaned in, concern on her face. "So the van…?"

Yvonne wanted to lay her head on the counter. "I don't even want to think about the van."

"But everyone's okay? No one was hurt— well, people, that is?"

Yvonne wiped her hands on a nearby towel and came around the counter. "That depends on your definition of *okay*. No one but Cecil's hurt more than bumps and bruises." It still felt ridiculous to call the dog by that name and recognize that Chaz had taken it in. "I just kept looking over at him, sitting there in Bruce's passenger seat with that dog piled on his lap, trying to figure out what had just happened." It was such an impulsive thing to do, and that man struck her as a long way from impulsive. Still, the compassion she'd seen from him impressed her as much as it had surprised her. Especially given the hours just before-hand. "I guess it was the last straw for him."

Kelly pulled the coffeepot from the brewer and poured a cup for herself, then refilled Yvonne's. "What do you mean?"

Sitting down at the front window tables, Yvonne gave a quick recap of the dinner and Hank's announcement.

"That sounds like a terrible thing to do. Who'd pit one son against the other like that?"

"That's what I think," Yvonne agreed. "And why on earth do it here, in front of me and Auntie P.? Hank is about to marry one of my favorite people in the whole world, and I'm worried. His actions are a huge red flag for me. I don't know how to tell her how I feel, or if I even should."

"Have you tried talking to her?"

"There wasn't really a time last night." Yvonne stifled another yawn. "But I plan to today. She told me something was coming, but she looked as uncomfortable as I felt when Hank announced it. The whole restaurant stared when Chaz blew up at his father. But really, can you blame the guy? I don't think Pauline knows what to do about it. I sure don't."

Kelly sipped her coffee. "Do you need me to drive you down into Asheville to a rental car company?"

"Let's wait until I hear what Ziggy has to say. I'm bracing myself that it won't be good news." She sat back and squinted her eyes shut. "I was only four payments away from being able to afford my first new van in the spring."

Kelly pasted on a hopeful smile. "Ziggy works wonders. Maybe it can be repaired."

"I think he was holding the van together for me as it was. I was counting on it making it through one more winter." When she'd first opened the shop, it seemed like everything had worked out perfectly. If God could bless a bakery, He'd blessed hers. Work was hard, but satisfying.

All that had somehow fizzled out in recent months. Now work was just hard. The joy of making brides happy had disappeared. That was why Auntie P.'s wedding seemed so important—it was a chance to get that spark back by baking the perfect wedding cake for someone she adored.

Instead, Pauline's fast and dramatic engagement to Hank Walker seemed to be clouding over with doubts. She didn't much like the man she saw in Hank last night. Could she trust Auntie P.'s heart to a man who'd cut one son clean out of the family land? Actually, letting Chaz manage it but not own it seemed even crueler. What was her role in all this supposed to be?

"You haven't gotten off to a good start with the Walker men, that's for sure."

"Hank seemed so nice yesterday. He looked—still looks—completely in love with Pauline. But this ranch inheritance thing. Wow. I don't know what to think."

"Chaz didn't strike me as a ray of sunshine even before all this." She gave Yvonne a look. "Then again, I remember saying that about Bruce when I first met him, too, and he turned out to be wonderful."

Yvonne didn't reply. Last night showed her layers in Chaz she hadn't thought were there. She couldn't decide how she felt about that.

Kelly raised an eyebrow. "Rather heroic to save an injured dog and take him in. He could have just left the dog with the vet. That's got to count for something, don't you think?"

Yvonne held up her hands. "Don't expect me to be able to figure this out today. I'm working on about four hours of sleep. I'm just glad Nancy's wedding isn't until tomorrow afternoon—I feel like I can barely make toast today."

The bell over the door rang, signaling the bakery's first customer of the day. "I'll let you go," Kelly said as she rose. "Do you want me to ask around town and see if anyone has a van you could borrow until you figure out what to do next? Or maybe Bruce's truck?"

Yvonne rose and waved to the neighbor coming through the door. "I only have to get the cake and cupcakes across the street to Hailey's. I'll manage."

Kelly hugged her. "Hang in there, okay? It'll work out."

Yvonne nodded and said, "Sure," but she didn't feel any confidence that it would. At least not anytime soon.

## Chapter Five

Cecil gave a low howl as he wobbled around the cabin's little kitchen.

"I hear you, buddy." Chaz frowned at the sad mug of instant coffee produced from the bottle he found in the cupboards. He dumped sugar into it and tried not to think of the much better coffee Yvonne must be brewing at Bliss Bakery. She made fabulous coffee. He took another sip and grimaced, thinking he'd had better from gas station vending machines. Still, caffeine was caffeine, and he needed it in any form. "At least you've got chow." He poured the packet of kibble out and set it down next to the bowl of water he'd just refilled. "Eat up. I'll head out and get some better stuff and gear in a bit."

Big grateful eyes looked up at him before Cecil ducked his nose into the food and began chewing noisily. Chaz considered the dog again, still a bit dumfounded he'd done what he'd done. *I own a dog. One I've got to figure out how to get back to Wander. What just happened?*

It struck Chaz that he'd found reason to ask that particular question often since being in Matrimony Valley. Right now he didn't have strong enough coffee to answer it. He wasn't sure strong enough coffee to answer that question even existed.

Cecil's 8:00 a.m. appointment with Dr. Mullins was in fifteen minutes, enough time for even Cecil's limping, comical gait to make it the three blocks to Puppy Love Veterinary Care. Honestly. The name made Chaz cringe more than the terrible coffee. The whole town's romance gimmick stumped him. Yvonne and even Bruce Lohan had told him how Mayor Jean had forgone her family's name to rechristen Matrim's Valley to Matrimony Valley in order to bring it back to life. It was an admirable—and clearly successful—idea, but too cheesy for him. Was Yvonne's cheerful, energetic personality fueled by living in such a constant state of hearts and flowers? Or could only someone with her outlook tolerate living here? And what was driving his curiosity about her, anyway?

Cecil wolfed down the last of his food, licking his chops with a satisfied slurp. Chaz downed the last of his coffee with nowhere near such enthusiasm, then slipped the makeshift leash over the dog's head and grabbed the cabin keys off the counter. "Off we go."

He took note—again—of the romance-themed business names as he and Cecil made their way down Aisle Avenue. There was a Love in Bloom Flower Shop, and a

Sweet Hearts Ice Cream Parlor, among others. Even the fishing outfitters he'd visited yesterday was called Catch Your Match, and, of course, the place where he'd been staying until last night was called Hailey's Inn Love.

The only store to evade a gooey name was Watson's Diner, which smelled delicious enough to make his stomach growl as he walked past. A hand-lettered sign gave him the welcome news that $3.99 would buy him two eggs, toast and coffee. The words *No Takeout* in red letters underneath, however, warned him it would have to wait. "I might need to head over there after we get you squared away," he told Cecil.

He'd give the town one thing: it was quiet and beautiful early in the morning. The mist hadn't yet burned off the mountainside, and the hints of spectacular fall colors were just starting to show.

He tried to ignore the fact that Yvonne's shop was already open. He told himself the urge to stop in was just because she would probably welcome Cecil inside for a minute while he got some great coffee and a doughnut.

It certainly couldn't be because of how he kept recalling her wide, frightened eyes those first few moments after the crash. Or the heartsick, mewling sound she'd made when they first came upon injured Cecil. Most of all, he couldn't seem to stop thinking about the warm, baffled look of surprise she gave him when he declared Cecil was coming home with him. *What just happened?* indeed.

Dr. Mullins was a nice enough guy, friendly and supportive of Chaz's impulsive dog acquisition. "Good-looking animal," he said, running his hands over the dog. "Underfed, so I expect he'll be grateful to you. And loyal."

*Loyal.* Now, there was a word that stuck in Chaz's throat this morning.

"I want to draw some blood, take another

X-ray, give him a thorough once-over and put a microchip in." Mullins flipped a page on his clipboard. "Let me keep him for an hour or two. You look like you could use breakfast and coffee. You probably passed Watson's. Wanda fries up a good egg."

Chaz gave Cecil a good pat. "I'll swing back for you in a bit." He took the wag of Cecil's tail as a sign of cooperation and promptly headed into Watson's Diner to wolf down a breakfast of his own.

Chaz devoured his food, bought a leash, collar and feeding bowls from the Have N Hold Home and Garden store, and then stared across the street. It was time to face Dad.

Yvonne stared out the window at Chaz. He was standing on the sidewalk, staring at the inn. Even from here, she could see his clenched fists.

She and Mama didn't really get along, but it had never been anything on the scale of what she'd seen last night. Mama never really voiced her vague disappointment. It just sort of leaked out.

She loved Janice and Rita, but Mama's boasts about how well they were doing had begun to bother Yvonne. She was ashamed at how tales of their shiny, admirable families and their successful husbands grated on her. *I chose to stay here. I love the valley and these people. I'm not sorry I didn't marry Neal, and I'm not incomplete just because I'm still alone. How is it Mama and my sisters can make me feel as if I've been left behind?*

She couldn't yet explain the unfamiliar need to do something else, go somewhere new. It made no sense given Bliss Bakery's moderate success. Still, the thought of gearing up next spring for another wedding season left her feeling weary rather than excited. And, when she was honest, entirely too single.

Was that why Chaz managed to capture

her attention? Yvonne watched Chaz's tall frame square itself for father-and-son battle. He looked strong and stomped on at the same time.

*God, bless that curmudgeon and his new dog.* The prayer surprised her. Pauline was a woman of faith and would never marry Hank if he wasn't, as well. Did that mean Chaz believed in God's sovereignty over a thorny situation like this? *I don't know where Chaz is going to go from here, so I hope You do.*

Even though part of him wanted to put a hundred miles between himself and his stepfather, Chaz crossed the street and headed up the stairs to Dad's hotel room. His anger seemed to boil back up with every step closer. They were going to have this out. Might as well do it here and now.

The door opened even before Chaz raised his fist to pound on it. Dad had bumped his head on the van's door pillar, and now a long black bruise arched over Dad's eye. It clashed with the wary look in the old man's eyes.

Dad shrugged as he caught Chaz's stare. "You should see the other guy." It was a standard crack they'd made anytime Chaz or Wyatt or anyone came home with a black eye. While Chaz had done it only a couple of times, Wyatt made it a regular habit.

The use of the family joke just made everything worse. "I am the other guy." Chaz made no attempt to lighten his words as he walked into the room.

"Would you have really socked me?" Dad's question needed no further explanation.

"Might've." It wasn't really true. It'd be lying to say the urge to haul off and punch his father hadn't risen up—he was that angry about the ranch's succession to Wyatt—but Chaz would never have actually hit the man. Even a betrayal this large couldn't untangle years of respect.

Well, not yet, at least.

"You sore?" Dad asked.

"Some."

"I expect so."

Suddenly Chaz wasn't sure why he'd come here. Dad had clearly made up his mind. What was the point in talking about it further?

"I kept the dog."

Dad scoffed. "You what?"

"I kept the dog. I have him here. Well, out in a cabin at Bruce Lohan's place because the inn doesn't take pets." Pets. He had a pet. Another wave of the *What just happened?* storm surrounding him lately.

Dad looked at him as if *that* was the most startling thing that had happened last night. "What are you going to do with a dog?"

Out of nowhere, a spurt of anger that Dad failed to recognize he'd always wanted a dog burned through Chaz's chest.

"Clearly not keep it on Wander, now, will I?" he shouted.

It was a stupid statement. Dad hadn't said a word about putting him off the land. As far as he knew, he was perfectly welcome to continue living in the house he called home. And Cecil, too, for that matter. As of last night, however, Chaz felt irrationally homeless. As if the land beneath his feet had been yanked out from under him—which wasn't so far off the truth.

"Settle down, Chaz. You're taking this wrong."

How else was he supposed to take this? Dad offered no explanation or defense. His silence told Chaz what he already knew: it was done. "Why?" He didn't bother to soften the edge of his tone.

Dad met his glare with a hard stare of his own. "It was time."

Chaz tossed the bag he'd been holding down on the coffee table. The bowls and leash clanged as they met the wood. He didn't apologize for the loud noise. He walked past his stepfather and stood in front of the windows that looked out over the town. The street scene was what most people would probably call charming, but right now Chaz found the whole place suffocatingly happy. His eyes wandered to the cheery window of Bliss Bakery. Matrimony Valley may be fine for the likes of Yvonne, but he couldn't stomach such an onslaught of happily-ever-afters. This place would only ever be the spot where his future imploded.

"I've been telling you it's time to handle the succession for years." Chaz turned back toward his stepfather. "So you pick here? Now?"

Dad's back stiffened. "You're telling me this would have been easier back in Colorado?"

The man had a point. Still… "In front of her? In front of both of them?"

Dad scratched his chin. "I doubt you'll understand this, but maybe I wanted to hand down the hardest decision of my life with the woman I love by my side."

Somehow that idea just made the whole thing worse. It connected him to Yvonne because he'd heard the toughest news of his life with her next to him at the table. The idea made his skin prickle.

Dad defiantly held his gaze. "You're stronger than how unfair you think this is."

*Unfair?* It was unfair that the man he had come to love like a father didn't know what that land meant to him. Unfair that Dad failed to realize that he wanted Wander Canyon Ranch more than anything else in life. Or—even worse—did know it and denied him ownership of the ranch anyway.

Out of nowhere, Chaz's mind raced back to the Sunday-school story of the prodigal son and the fit thrown by the loyal son at the party thrown for the wayward one. *Unfair* was absolutely the right word.

Chaz jabbed a finger at his stepfather. "Wyatt can't do it, Dad."

He waited for Dad to argue that, but instead Dad sighed in agreement. "Not without you he can't. Not yet." To Chaz's surprise, he added, "But you could do it without Wyatt, couldn't you?"

What on earth was that supposed to mean? As far as Chaz was concerned, he'd been running the ranch half without Wyatt from the start. He wanted to shout "Absolutely!" Only that seemed to be exactly what Dad wanted to hear, and Chaz wasn't about to give him that satisfaction right now.

"I could," he muttered instead.

"I know that."

Chaz glared at him. "This isn't right. None of it."

"I know you see it that way."

Dad's simplistic answers were infuriating. "I should just get on a plane back to Wander right now."

"I hope you don't."

Chaz wanted a fight. He wanted to have it out with his dad right now, to yell and argue and maybe even throw something. The low boil that had started in his chest last night at dinner was itching to spill over and do damage. There was probably a very good reason Hank put a thousand miles between him and Wyatt right now—Chaz couldn't say what he'd do to his infuriating half brother if he was within arm's reach at the moment.

Chaz paced the room, flexing and fisting his hands while his breath came in pants worthy of Cecil.

Dad planted his feet in the center of the room. "Go walk it off, Chaz."

How dare Dad spout advice like that? Treat this massive injustice like a temper tantrum in the horse corral or some minor spat between him and Wyatt? *You don't just walk it off when someone yanks your future right out from under you,* he wanted to shout.

To Chaz's amazement, Dad opened the hotel room door and motioned him out.

"Seriously?"

Dad stood his ground. "I've made my decision. I know you don't like it, and I didn't expect you to. So go walk it off."

Chaz glared right back.

Dad said nothing, only met Chaz's angry eyes. He was being dismissed. Chaz was thirty years old and he couldn't remember the last time Dad told him what to do with that tone in his voice. The old man was changing in ways that bugged him beyond comprehension. Chaz knew the stubborn set of that jaw, and knew that when Hank Walker made up his mind about something, you might as well carve it in stone.

So while he was steamed, and wanted to yell half a dozen things no son should ever yell at his father—stepdad or not—Chaz simply bit down on his tongue until it hurt, grabbed the bag off the coffee table and stalked out the open door.

He didn't bother to say goodbye for fear of what else would come out behind the word.

## Chapter Six

Yvonne held her breath as she stood beside Ziggy. Together they stared at the crumpled vehicle that had once been her bakery van. Ziggy resettled his baseball cap and gave a low whistle. "Nope. She's a goner."

Ziggy's Valley Garage was one of the few businesses no one even considered renaming in the transformation from Matrim's Valley to Matrimony Valley. Not only was Ziggy's a memorable name, but no one had yet come up with a decently marriage-related garage name—although Mayor Jean had bemoaned a few horrid contenders. Not one person on the town council could ever stomach suggesting "The Marriage Carriage" to Jerome Zigler, so Ziggy's Valley Garage stayed Ziggy's.

Yvonne would have swallowed any ridiculous name if it had meant Ziggy gave her better news about her van. "You're sure? You know I only had four more payments." She moaned. "I was so looking forward to buying a new one in the spring."

Ziggy nodded at the dented vehicle. "Gonna have to buy a new one *now*, I guess." He shrugged. "Got good insurance?"

"I have insurance."

*Good* was not the word that came to mind an hour ago when she ended her thirty-minute phone conversation with her insurance company. "But they won't pay out enough for me to get a new one." By the spring, she would have put away enough to be able to get a nice shiny new van.

Now the only van she could afford to buy would have to be another used one. It was hard to trust God would provide after such a double whammy of misfortune. This morning she couldn't seem to muster enough faith to overpower the disappointed ache in her stomach.

"Tough break." The mechanic put a commiserating hand on her shoulder. "I'll keep an eye out for a bargain, if you like."

All of North Carolina likely didn't hold the bargain she'd need to meet this new challenge. "Thanks. I'd appreciate that." With a resigned sigh, Yvonne held out her hand.

"Here you go." Ziggy gave her the plastic bag she'd seen him holding as she walked up, the sight that told her the van was totaled even before the man spoke one word.

Ziggy's strange ritual for goner cars was as much a part of town legend as the falls: when a car was declared totaled or dead, Ziggy would remove all the lug nuts from the wheels and hand them to the grieving customer like an undertaker handing over last personal effects. Valley residents would take the bag out back to the river that ran behind town and ceremoniously throw the lug nuts into the water in an odd ritual of farewell.

Everybody knew it was ridiculous, but everybody did it anyway. Yvonne often wondered just how large the pile of metal remembrances was down there at the bottom of the river. The thought that she was about to add to that pile settled hard as iron in her soul.

Her face must have shown the despair. "I can take ten dollars off the tow fee if you'll bring by another box of doughnuts tomorrow morning," he offered.

She had brought Ziggy a dozen doughnuts today as a thank-you for coming halfway to Asheville to pick up her van—or what was left of it—at no extra charge. That was one of the best things about the valley. Everybody looked out for everybody else. Even when her yearning for a life beyond the valley pulled as hard as it had this year, Yvonne could talk herself out of it by remembering this community. After all, how could she ever be sure the rest of the world held folks like Ziggy? Or Jean, or Kelly?

Such wondering didn't matter because now she surely couldn't afford to do anything but stay here. *I should feel planted, Lord, but I feel stuck.* Taking the bag, Yvonne left the garage with leaden steps. She turned her feet toward the river, steeling herself to toss the van's "remains"—and what felt like any dreams of a bigger future—to their watery grave. She doubted tossing the sixteen metal pieces into the river would make her feel better. This morning her future seemed as totaled as the vehicle.

The sound of shouting stopped her a few yards back from the riverbank. Bursts of angry noise made her wonder if she was interrupting a fight of some kind, but the sound of something large hitting the water after each grunt made her curious.

She slowed down, keeping to the bushes until the curving shallow bank of the river came into view.

Chaz Walker stood there, hurling rocks into the water like grenades.

Cecil sat dutifully beside him, as if the two had been dog and owner for years instead of hours. Yvonne watched Chaz pick up another sizable rock, growl like an angry bear and send it flying into the water. While he uttered no words, she could hear the roar of his anger from her position by the trees.

There was someone else in town this morning who felt their future had been totaled. Yvonne believed lives didn't intersect by chance, but why Chaz? Why now?

He threw two more rocks while she watched, and when he picked up a third, she turned to leave and come back another time. The sound of the rock hitting the bank with a defeated thud stopped her. She turned back toward the river to see Chaz just standing there, empty-handed, staring into the water. The set of his shoulders was pure hopeless frustration—much like hers, but then again, so much larger. After all, her loss was a van. Chaz had lost his claim to the place he called home. The lug nuts in her hands suddenly felt lighter than the large rock Chaz had let fall at his feet.

Cecil wobbled up to a stand—no easy task with the cast on his hind leg—and nudged up against Chaz. The silent show of friendship rose a lump in Yvonne's throat, and she knew she couldn't walk away.

"Good choice," she called softly as she stepped out of the shade of the path and into the sunshine on the grassy riverbank. "Big rocks for big problems, my dad always said."

Cecil turned and offered a woof of greeting. While Chaz startled a bit at her entrance, he mostly seemed too spent to care. It was just before noon, and the sheen of sweat on his face made Yvonne wonder just how long he'd been out here.

She walked toward him, holding out the bag in her hands. "Want to see how far you can send one of these?"

Chaz squinted in confusion at the contents. "Lug nuts?"

"Ziggy at the garage gives them to you to toss in the river when your car dies."

He gave her exactly the look she'd expect from him at an oddball explanation like that. "You have to know how weird that sounds."

Yvonne opened the bag and pulled one out. "Maybe it's not so weird. I mean, what do rocks accomplish when you throw them?"

"Less harm than punches," he said. There was something close to a shadow of a grin on his face. She'd never really seen him smile. He looked like he would have a handsome smile, but she doubted she'd ever get the chance to know.

"Still mad at your stepfather?" It was a silly question given the magnitude of what had happened last night.

Chaz nodded toward the lug nut. "If I told you I expect I could send this into Tennessee, does that answer your question?"

So he did have a tiny bit of humor in there somewhere. She handed the nut to him. "Let's see."

Chaz considered the nugget of metal for a moment. He then tossed it between his hands as if measuring its weight. With a final nod toward her, he turned toward the water, wound back his arm with a startling power and sent the shiny silver piece sailing what looked like miles upstream.

Crazy as it was, there really was a small zing of satisfaction to watching it fly in a sparkling arc. She did feel a tiny burst of closure as it dunked into the water with a resolute splash. Cecil barked and wagged his tail.

"Hmm," she said, unsure of what comment to make. She settled for "Impressive."

He gave her a dubious look before saying, "Your turn."

Yvonne selected a nut, made a silly show of hefting it like Chaz had done and then sent it into the river perhaps a dozen yards away. While her throw was smaller by far in scale, the launch felt just as satisfying. She almost managed a laugh when Cecil barked an equal approval of her effort.

"What do you know?" she offered. "It does make you feel better." She gave Cecil a generous pat before pulling another lug nut from the bag. "Have another go."

"Oh, no." He raised his hands as if to say *I'm not getting involved in your crazy traditions.* "They're *your* ceremonial lug nuts."

An actual joke. From Chaz Walker. She let herself enjoy the much-needed laughter. "But I like how far you can throw them." She did. There was something about having the strength of him nearby, even last night, even amid his own pain. He seemed the sort to always stand steady while she felt as if she'd topple over at any moment.

She narrowed one eye at him, daring a bit of playfulness. "Think you can beat that last throw?"

There it was—the tiniest glimpse of a mischievous glint in his eye. He shifted his stance and raised one eyebrow. "Are you asking me for a personal-best dead-car lug-nut throw?"

She couldn't help but like him. Just a bit. Sure, they were still at odds over Hank and Pauline, and the small tug she felt might be more commiseration than anything else. But for just this moment, here and now, Chaz Walker was the perfect antidote to all that was going wrong.

"As a matter of fact, I'm asking for a world-record dead-car lug-nut throw." She plunked the scratched chrome piece into his hands, her fingertips brushing his calloused palm.

A split second of *what?* flashed between them before Chaz gave the nut a small toss or two. "World record?" he repeated, the mischievous look growing.

Was it odd to enjoy this? With him? "Epic," she found herself replying. "Downright legendary."

Their eyes connected for something that felt far too long before Chaz sent the piece of metal flying upstream a second time. An actual smile made it to his face when the nut splashed into the water perhaps a dozen yards farther than his first throw. Yes, Chaz Walker did indeed have a handsome smile. Rare, but handsome. Even Cecil offered a *woof* of congratulations.

Chaz turned to her. "Satisfied?"

"Surprisingly," she replied, meaning it. She'd have to eat her words about Ziggy's strange tradition after today. "Not that it helps with tomorrow's wedding. Besides, I've got too much baking to do for Nancy's reception to go down to Asheville to the rental car agency before then."

Tomorrow's wedding was another reason Pauline and Hank were in town. Nancy was a family friend, and their attendance at the event was supposed to have been an informal introduction of sorts of Hank to the family. Now her whole family would see how she couldn't afford to replace the damaged van. The weekend just kept getting better.

"So how will you deliver the cake?"

"I only have to get everything across the street to Hailey's inn." She shrugged. "I'll get some help to make it work."

"I can give you a hand with that."

She couldn't have been more surprised. "You?"

"Seeing as I wrecked your car, it's the least I can do."

"I don't blame you for what happened to my van." She nodded toward Cecil. "Or him."

"I was behind the wheel when it happened."

Her van was not his fault. "You were *helping* me by being behind the wheel. I'm pretty sure if I had been behind the wheel, things would have been worse."

He kicked at a rock with his boot. "Your van is totaled. We're already at *worse*."

Chaz's sense of obligation was sweet, but misguided. "A lot worse could have happened. Someone could have gotten hurt. Or Cecil could have—" she searched for a kind way to put it "—not made it. You don't owe me anything."

He stepped a bit closer, lowering his voice as if they weren't alone. "You'd be helping me, actually. I'm in no hurry to be a guest at this thing tomorrow. Dad and Pauline dragged me into it as it is, and after last night it's the last place I want to be. If I say I have to help you, then maybe I can beg off going to the ceremony and reception."

Shuttling the cake and dessert table sweets would be easier with another strong set of hands, and most of the valley residents were already busy with their own roles in making weddings happen. And, startling as it was, she was finding Chaz Walker rather nice to have around. When they weren't arguing, that was. Which, at the moment, they weren't.

"Okay, then, mister, you got yourself a deal. Be at the shop at ten in the morning. You'll have to leave Cecil at home."

He nodded. "Got it. Thanks."

She wasn't quite sure why it felt strange to say "You're welcome." After a pause, she made herself say, "I appreciate the help. So," she said as she fingered another of the lug nuts. "Now that we've solved part of my problem, how about you? Feel any better?"

The amusement left his face at the reference to his own predicament. He shifted his gaze to the river, stuffing his hands in his pockets. "My problem takes more than hurling lug nuts to solve."

Maybe she could return the favor and

stand by him in his own problem. "I'm sorry about what's happened with the ranch."

"You and me both."

She dared to say what she'd been thinking all night. "It doesn't seem right. What Hank did."

His whole body tensed at the words. "I'll say," he grumbled. "He wasn't like this before. I've tried to get him to talk about succession issues for years."

"Why now, then?"

"I've been asking myself the same question." He pierced her with a glare that held none of the ease of their moments before. "And I only come up with one answer. Your aunt."

She practically dropped the bag of lug nuts. "You think Pauline did this?"

"Do you have another explanation?" The sharpness in his eyes told her she'd just tipped the lid off the boiling pot of his anger. He began pacing the riverbank. "Suddenly Pauline comes into the picture and he goes off and makes this wild decision. Handing Wander Canyon Ranch down to Wyatt? This isn't him. I don't know how or why, but he wouldn't do this before. So it's got to be Pauline."

That was a ridiculous idea. "My aunt didn't have anything to do with what Hank decided."

"How would you know? Things were fine before her. Maybe not perfect, but good. Headed in the right direction. Now this mess."

Chaz's words made Yvonne realize she didn't actually know. She couldn't say for a fact that Auntie P. hadn't been somehow involved in the decision. Except for one thing: "This doesn't sound like anything my auntie P. would ever think to do."

"Yeah, well, my stepfather's been doing things I didn't think he'd ever do. He's acting strange. He's someone I don't even recognize. Come on… *Paris?*" The edge in his tone made Cecil sit back down and the hair on the back of Yvonne's neck stand up.

Pauline deserved Paris. She'd wanted a Paris honeymoon for as long as Yvonne could remember. "Where they honeymoon," she said through gritted teeth as she tried to keep a lid on her own mood, "is not your call."

"No," he fired back, "because it's all Pauline's call. She had to put him up to this. She's got to be what's changed him. The Hank Walker I know wouldn't…" Chaz didn't finish the sentence, just picked up the rock he'd let fall earlier and sent it flying into the water with a fierce growl. Cecil offered no bark of approval this time, just silent, cautious attention.

*Give the family ranch to your brother*, Yvonne finished in her head for him. It lit fire to the doubt that had kept her awake last night as much as the demise of her car. *What kind of man does that to his sons?*

"Look, I don't know why Hank made that inheritance choice…"

"Succession," he corrected without even looking at her. Neal used to correct her all the time, and it pushed her buttons as sharply then as it did now.

Yvonne stalked over to stand in front of him. "Pauline is *not* behind what your stepfather did. *He* is. Don't you go blaming Pauline for Hank's favoritism. And I have to say I don't much care for the way your stepdad runs his family. The family my aunt Pauline's about to become part of. So maybe you're not the only one worried about what happens next."

She hadn't meant for it to come out quite so fiercely, but Chaz Walker seemed to draw an argument out of her like breathing. Hank's actions made no sense to her. They seemed downright mean-spirited. No loving man would repay a son's—even a stepson's—loyalty with such a bitter deal. "So I'll say this. After last night, I'm not so

big on the idea of Pauline marrying someone capable of doing what your dad just
did to you."

Chaz's face blazed in anger. "Oh, so now
your aunt's too good for my dad. Is that it?"

"Maybe," she fired back, the tension of
the past twenty-four hours slipping her temper out of control.

"Well, I tell you, this is all her doing from
where I sit." He pointed at her. "There's no
other explanation."

"Except that maybe you're just finding
out what kind of man your dad really is."
How had she let him goad her to the point
of shouting? "Maybe it's better we all see
this before things got permanent."

"So now you don't want them to get married. Is that what you're saying?"

Yvonne's vague sense of doubt crystal-
lized into conviction at Chaz's harsh words.
She pushed the volume of her voice back
down, fingers tightening around the bag of
lug nuts. "I'm worried, yes."

Chaz jumped on that. "You don't fool me. You've had doubts the whole time. You just were afraid to face them. 'I think it's brave.' Not exactly an endorsement, is it?"

He was so aggravating. "If you think Auntie P. has such an irrational hold on Hank, why don't you go ask her why she'd talk him into something like this?"

"Maybe I should," he barked back.

She pointed in the direction of her house, where Pauline was staying. "I live at 42 Bouquet Circle, three blocks up. The stone house with the green door. Go ask my sweet, loving aunt why she thinks it's such a fine idea to do something so awful to you."

She wasn't keen on sending Chaz to her house, nor did she cherish the idea of foisting this angry bear of a man onto Auntie P., but if Chaz talked to her, maybe he would realize he was laying blame where it definitely didn't belong.

"Talk to Pauline?" He scoffed, leaning down to pick up Cecil's leash. She hated how the dog's puzzled eyes showed a twinge of fear at their raised voices, but the man was way off base in his thinking. "What would that solve? About as much as throwing those lug nuts in the water, if you ask me."

"It actually helped," she fired back, shaking the bag at him.

Chaz threw his free hand in the air. "You're all nuts. This whole town is off its rocker. I don't know what Dad sees in any of you." With the sharp command "Come!" he turned toward the path and began walking at a pace that the poor injured dog was hard-pressed to match. Thankfully, after half a dozen strides, Chaz realized it and, while still bristling with anger, slowed his pace for the dog.

"Where do you think you're going?" It was a stupid question, given that she'd just told him where to go, but she wasn't about to let his insult of the whole town be the final word here.

"To talk to Pauline. Find out what on earth is going on here. And just maybe tell her what I really think of her."

*Watch yourself, cowboy,* Yvonne snarled in her mind. *She just might tell you what she really thinks of you.*

As Chaz and Cecil made their slow-speed stomp back onto the path, Yvonne piled all the remaining lug nuts into her hand and sent them flying into the water.

# Chapter Seven

"I was wondering when you'd show up," Pauline said as she pulled the green door open to the small cozy house on Bouquet Circle. She narrowed her light blue eyes—nearly the same color as Yvonne's, so it must be a family trait. She tilted her chin boldly up at him in the same way Yvonne did, as well. "That's quite a knock you've got there."

Chaz had to admit that given his current mood, it probably did sound more like a pound. He'd tried to calm himself down the whole walk back to deposit Cecil at the cabin and come here, but it hadn't done one lick of good. He was steamed and ready for a fight, while she just looked at him with the continual calm good nature he'd always found hard to swallow. The woman let too much of life just roll off her back, as if she didn't take everything that was happening seriously.

Well, he took all this very seriously, and she was going to hear about it. He stood there for a minute, deciding which of the angry thoughts storming through his head to say first.

Pauline merely clasped her hands in front of her like a patient schoolmarm. "Where's your new canine companion?"

So she'd talked to Hank. It shouldn't surprise him one bit. "Back at the cabin where I'm staying." He should ask where Dad was, but at the moment he didn't much care. Unlike last night's fiasco, he wanted to have this conversation one-on-one.

"I take it you've got a thing or two to say."

"Yes, I do." It bugged him that in the

space of ten seconds she'd already managed to defuse some of the anger he'd built up on his way over here.

Arriving at some sort of decision, Pauline nodded, then turned and reached for the cardigan sweater hanging from the coatrack just behind her. "This sounds to me like an outdoor conversation."

He thought it more of an indoor, private interrogation than an outdoor conversation, but Pauline just swept past him. "Pull the door shut, Chaz, honey, and let's go talk this out over by the falls."

*Don't you "Chaz, honey" me*, he growled inside his head while he pulled Yvonne's door shut and followed her down the road. How did she do that? That tiny woman somehow just stole control of this conversation from him. *Annoying* didn't even begin to cover it. "Easy to see where Yvonne gets it," he mumbled to himself.

"Didn't quite catch that," she called sweetly as she put her arms through the sleeves.

He merely grunted and picked up the pace. He came around past her on the sidewalk and then turned back to square off at her. "You really want to do this outside?"

She headed right around him on the sidewalk and kept walking. "I always find it's best. God's wide-open skies tend to lend perspective. And the falls are so calming." She gave him a glance over her shoulder that roughly translated to *which you clearly need.*

Chaz did not want to calm down. He didn't want to walk it off. How everyone but Yvonne expected him to sit back and swallow the injustice of the ranch going to Wyatt infuriated him. It couldn't be a done deal. He wouldn't let it be a done deal. This was not going down without a fight, happy wedding town or no.

When they arrived at the falls, Pauline took a seat on the bench that faced the water. She folded her hands in her lap and looked up at him attentively. Looked up, because he refused to sit. He stood. Or more precisely, paced the grass in front of her. There were a dozen things clamoring to come out of his mouth, so he dived in with the one pushing hardest.

"You've changed my dad." He was a tiny bit proud for not saying "You ruined my dad."

"I believe I have." Just when he was glad for the agreement, she added, "That's what love is supposed to do to us, isn't it?"

Time for the gloves to come off. "Was last night your idea?"

She thought for a moment before responding, "In a way, yes."

"So it *was* you who got him to leave the ranch to Wyatt. I knew it."

"Well, no."

She met his stare, letting that sink in before continuing. "The succession plan was your father's idea. But I did suggest he bring you here to tell you."

"Why?" The single word had been burning a hole in his chest all night long.

"Seems to me you already know that. You two would have ended up in a knock-down-drag-out had he told you alone back on the ranch. I'm not sure I would have done it at a restaurant like that, but it did keep things from getting out of hand."

"Seriously?" How could anyone endorse how Dad had done what he'd done?

"And had you been back in Colorado, I expect you'd have stomped off and found Wyatt and had it out with him, as well. This was better for everyone."

"Everyone?" he blasted back before turning away from her. *Not me. Not even close.*

Her voice came from behind him. "Would it surprise you to know I think it's unfair? Because I do."

Chaz barely registered Pauline's question. He was too busy trying to keep her comment about it being better for everyone from choking him. The searing sense of betrayal seemed to be in every corner of his chest.

There was no way on God's green earth this plan was better for everyone, least of all him.

"Hank explained to me how it all works. Or is supposed to work." He heard Pauline's voice continue behind him. "He gave me loads of reasons why the land is more valuable undivided. It being in the family for generations and all. The whole Walker bloodline bit I expect you've heard before. So I understand the facts of it. I see your father's point of view."

She came around to stand in front of Chaz. "But I place the value of an undivided family—*your* undivided family—above all those acres."

The startling words pierced the fog of Chaz's anger. Wait—Pauline *wasn't* in favor of leaving the ranch intact to Wyatt? She *didn't* agree with what Dad had decided?

"We actually had a pretty good row about

it, Hank and I." Pauline made a *tsk*-ing sound, shaking her head. "But I don't think I have to tell you your father is a stubborn man. Even more stubborn than you are— which is saying something."

While Chaz was resistant and even downright suspicious of Pauline, the one thing he did like about her was the way she referred to Hank as "your father." He appreciated that she shunned the distinction of the stepfather title he'd never liked. This morning, however, her use of the word *father* just seemed to twist the knife already lodged in his chest.

"But the land belongs to him," she said. "It's ultimately his decision."

The words and the challenging way Pauline looked at him reminded him all too much of Yvonne. Was every woman in this family equally as exasperating?

"So no matter what you may think," she went on, "it wasn't my idea. It wasn't my decision. He'd been avoiding the subject—

just like you said—because he knew what it would do to you boys. The only thing I'm guilty of here is asking him to settle the matter before we were married. He thought this was the softest way to deliver a mighty hard piece of news."

"That doesn't make you on my side." The words felt bitter and childish as they left his mouth. With the exception of those first few minutes earlier with Yvonne—peaceful, amusing moments that dissolved all too fast into yet another argument—the past few hours he'd felt like last night's careening van. A slammed and leaking thing, doomed to watch his future bleed out while everyone stood around and watched.

"I'm not on your side, Chaz. I'm not on anybody's side except Hank's. If anything, I'm trying to be on everybody's side."

Her platitudes stabbed at him. "There is no 'everybody's side' here. There's no happy medium. He chose Wyatt over me, plain and simple."

"He did not choose Wyatt over you. He recognized your strength over Wyatt's..." She shook her head and waved a hand. "Well, I hate to say *weakness* but..."

He was unable to take any more. "Don't sit there and make this what it isn't."

Pauline stilled, and her glare was as sharp as his tone. "What isn't it?"

The list came barreling out of him. "It isn't okay. Or fair. It's not the right thing to do. Or anything even remotely good for Wander Canyon Ranch. Or me. Or probably even Wyatt. Dad would never have done this in his right mind if he weren't..."

Pauline stood, planting her hands on her hips. "In love and planning for a future different from what you had in mind? Facing an issue he's dodged too long? So long it's about to start an all-out war between the two people he loves most in the world?"

"He's making the biggest mistake of his life!" He'd spent the last three months trying not to say those words. A long silence hung between them, one even the roar of the waterfall couldn't drown out.

"Well," she said softly. He couldn't make out if her tone was one of hurt or resignation, which just made it worse. "You finally said it out loud."

When he dared to look at her, she had returned to her seat but still met his gaze with an unnerving directness. "It's been practically radiating out of your pores since Hank and I started up together. Give me a little credit for perceptiveness here. In return, I'll give you a little credit for not yelling that at the dinner table last night."

Chaz remained silent, unsure of how to respond.

"Your father and I are not a mistake." Pauline said each word slowly, giving it weight. She crossed her arms over her chest and sat back. "And I might even be able to prove it to you."

"How?" he asked.

"Could that stubborn brain of yours crack

open just wide enough to consider there might be a third option to how to hand down the ranch?"

He'd spent most of last night racking his brain on the same issue. He'd researched succession strategies for the past two years. She couldn't possibly contrive a solution where he didn't see one.

"You have an idea?"

Pauline didn't back down. "No, I don't. But that doesn't mean there isn't one out there. I love your father. Very much. Enough to want every part of his life to be at peace. Including you and Wyatt. So I intend to nudge Hank to keep looking, keep thinking on it. While I recognize it is Hank's call, I still think it's a bad idea and I'm praying every day for a better one to come along. Course, if you'd rather I stopped those efforts…"

"No." The single word made him feel like he'd just surrendered something, although he couldn't rightly say what.

"And could you widen that crack just a bit to make room for the thought that I might just hold a useful amount of sway with your father at the moment? One that might be helpful against the stubborn nature you both share?" She narrowed her eyes. "You're related to that man in more ways than you think, Chaz."

So many people said that. For years friends and family would remark how Chaz was more like Hank than Wyatt ever was. He'd always been secretly proud of that. Now the similar traits just made the whole current predicament that much worse.

To his surprise, Pauline stood up, walked right up to him and held out her hand. "Truce?"

Join forces with Pauline? Ally himself with the woman he'd stopped just short of saying was ruining his father? He hated the idea.

But he was also fresh out of other options. Even though every cell in his body seemed to clash at the idea, he held out his hand and said, "Truce."

Yvonne did what any woman would do who'd just had her car declared dead, had her town insulted, had a mountain of work ahead of her, couldn't sort out her feelings about the furious man she'd just sent toward Pauline and had just admitted to doubting that same aunt's impending marriage.

She decided to go get ice cream.

She grabbed her phone and texted MN? to Jean, hoping the new mom would welcome a spontaneous treat at Marvin's Sweet Hearts Ice Cream Parlor just down the street. The MN? was a shorthand she, Jean and Kelly had developed that stood for "I'm going to *Marvin's Now*—wanna come?"

Fussy baby, Jean typed back, adding a frowning emoji to her text.

Fussy ME, Yvonne replied. Come anyway.

15 min came across her screen, making Yvonne smile. Jean was the perfect person

to help her sort through the knots of her life at the moment. Even though Jean was only a few years older, a challenging life—including the death of her father, launching Matrimony Valley and the father of her adorable deaf son, Jonah, showing up as the brother to the valley's first bride—had given her wisdom and grace beyond her years. Ice cream and Jean could make any situation better, not to mention the chance to hold sweet baby Julia, even if fussy.

She ducked back into the bakery, where Cathy Bolton was wiping down countertops. "How'd you like to get started on mixing cake batter for tomorrow's wedding for me? I need another thirty minutes."

Cathy, who had started as counter help but was showing a real talent for baking, grinned. "Absolutely. The yellow cake, right? I can get started on the raspberry filling, too, if you like."

She'd never let someone else make a Bliss cake before, but she'd never been in this much of a bind before, either. She'd be back from Marvin's before the layers even came out of the oven. "Text me if you get stuck."

Cathy nodded. "I won't."

She headed out the door—and practically ran headlong into Chaz Walker. She bumped hard into his shoulder and they both stepped back fast from the accidental closeness.

"I'm just heading out…" She stopped herself from revealing her ice cream run, suspecting Chaz would never take to something so impulsive and frivolous for stress reduction. Whatever camaraderie they had found back at the creek was long gone.

"Your aunt sent me. I'm supposed to tell you she wants us to meet with her and Hank and the pastor at the church. One o'clock, before he has to do the rehearsal for the other wedding." The small spark she'd seen in his eyes was nowhere to be found. In fact, he sounded like he'd rather be anywhere than in a church with Hank and Pauline…and her?

Some tiny part of her missed the man she'd met at the riverbank, but there was no way to go back with all the issues pulling at them now. Given the last time the four of them had been together, she wasn't that eager to get them all together again. "Why?"

He wheeled around, one hand to his hair. "Do I look like I know?"

"Well, you just talked to her, so you must know something."

"Believe me, I don't have a clue what's going on here. Pauline just told me to come tell you to be at the church at one. Your guess is as good as mine." He turned to start walking in the direction of Kelly's cottage.

"What did Doc Mullins say about Cecil?" she called after him, not wanting them to end on a sour note again.

He turned back toward her. "He's fine,"

he said, reaching for a softer tone. "Well, close to fine. A bit underweight, up to date on all his shots now, and the leg should heal up right."

"Nobody's come looking for him?" She found herself genuinely worried that Chaz might have to give the dog back if its rightful owner showed. He and the dog seemed to need each other. Doc Mullins believed in animal rescues. He said God always sent the right furry companion to the right soul at the right time.

"No. He's mine."

Chaz's instantaneous decision to take on Cecil seemed so wildly out of character for a man like him. Still, the way he'd held on to that dog in the car on the way into the valley wouldn't leave her memory. "He's lucky to have you, then. He seems like a great companion."

A puzzled look filled Chaz's features. "How do you stand it?"

The question took her aback. "Stand what?"

He gestured up and down the street. "The whole place. An entire town bent on pairing folks up. It's all over everything. Everyone is married or getting married. Doesn't it bug you? Make you feel as if it's some sort of fault to be single?"

Never before this month had she been bothered by her unmarried status in a town dedicated to marriage. It irked her that he'd somehow picked up on it. To cover herself, she gave him her best *you've got to be kidding me* glare. "Did your mother teach you to be this charming?"

At least he looked a bit remorseful at the sharp way he'd put it. "I didn't mean it that way."

"I was engaged once." Even as she felt her chin jut out in defiance, she felt foolish for letting him goad that fact out of her in the middle of Aisle Avenue. "I ended it," she added, just so he'd know she hadn't been dumped.

He seemed to grapple with what to say

to that, finally ending up with a mumbled "I'm sorry."

"I'm not," she countered more sharply than she would have liked. Then she added, "He was a little too much like you."

# *Chapter Eight*

Yvonne was so unnerved by her conversation with Chaz that she was halfway through devouring her turtle sundae by the time Jean and baby Julia arrived.

Marvin set down the glass he was wiping. "Mornin', Mayor Jean. And our newest little citizen." He broke into the warm smile that made Marvin everyone's unofficial grandpa in the valley. Everybody loved Marvin, and Marvin loved everybody right back. Aside from his delicious creations, Yvonne considered Marvin one of the best things about Matrimony Valley.

"Morning, Marvin." Jean's voice was as

weary as her eyes. "Hope you don't mind a little crying." As if on cue, Julia began fussing.

"I've seen far worse. Your regular?"

Marvin knew Jean favored mocha milkshakes, just like he knew Yvonne favored turtle sundaes. Marvin knew the favorites of just about everyone in town.

"Soon as I get that shake fixed," Marvin said, "I'll take the little one off your hands so's you can sip in peace." When another cry erupted from Julia, he winked and added, "Well, something close to peace."

As he scooped out the coffee and chocolate ice cream, the older man asked a little too casually, "Was that Hank Walker's boy I saw you talking to, Yvonne?"

Jean gave Yvonne a knowing look as she settled herself and Julia into the table by the window. "And here I thought that sundae was about Ziggy declaring your car a goner." Always quick with solutions, Jean narrowed her eyes in thought. "You've only got tomorrow's wedding and your aunt's yet to do till the holidays—could you get by with a rental van?"

"Maybe. Kelly had the same thought." Yvonne spooned a big helping of ice cream into her mouth and let the creamy taste ease off all the sharp edges Chaz Walker had brought up in her chest.

"So it's not just the van."

"Well, no."

Marvin set down a tall glass complete with a dollop of whipped cream and a cherry in front of Jean. "I expect it's about that run-in she just had with the son of the groom." Before Yvonne could contradict him, Marvin held out his hands for the baby. "Okay, little one, let's you and I take a tour of the back room."

After she handed off Julia to Marvin, Jean took a long moment to savor her first sip. "Let's hear it."

Yvonne gave her a quick rundown of dinner, Hank's devastating announcement, the crash, Cecil and the scene down by the river. While she left out the tangle of feelings she had for Chaz Walker, it was gratifying to see Jean stunned at what Hank had done. "Why would a father do that? Set sons against each other like that?"

"Search me. But, of course, Chaz thinks Pauline put Hank up to this."

Jean shook her head. "That doesn't make any sense to me."

"Me neither, and I sent him over to my house so Pauline could set him straight. I don't think that happened." With a start, Yvonne realized she'd never gotten as far as asking how the conversation had gone. It seemed as if she and Chaz couldn't say three sentences to each other without getting into an argument.

"I sure hope Hank's worth marrying into a mess like that." Jean was speaking from experience. Years ago she'd walked away from an engagement to her now-husband, Josh, because of vicious family entanglements as well as Josh's former workaholic tendencies. Would God grant Auntie P. the same happy ending He'd worked for Josh and Jean?

Yvonne dared to say it. "I'm not sure he is."

Jean set down the milkshake. "Are you saying you don't think Pauline should marry Hank?"

"I don't know. It's been so fast. I'd swallowed all my doubts because she seemed so incredibly happy."

"They both do. I was giving them a tour of the falls the other day and they were holding hands and gazing at each other like goofy teenagers."

"I know." She'd had the same joyful reaction when first seeing Hank and Pauline together. "But what I saw at the restaurant sent up a load of red flags. I mean, what do we really know about this guy? Auntie P.'s usually a smart cookie, but what if her feelings are blinding her to warning signs?"

If the unsettling hints of attraction she felt for Chaz made it hard to think clearly, what must Pauline's head-over-heels affection for Hank do to her sense of logic?

"I get that you're concerned," Jean said carefully. "But are you sure it's any of your business? They're two grown adults. If Pauline thinks it's worth it to wade into that fray, do you have any right to stop her?"

The words sounded so much like the speech she'd given to Chaz. Easy words to say when she was the one in favor of the union. "Chaz called marrying Pauline the biggest mistake of his father's life. What if this is as big a mistake for Pauline? Don't you think I should at least say something?"

Jean sighed. "She's a woman in love. She might not listen."

Yvonne groaned and ate some more ice cream. She'd never told Jean—or Kelly, or anyone but Auntie P., for that matter—the real reason she'd called it off with Neal. Now wasn't the time to go into that shameful story. She'd let love—or what she thought was love—blind her to Neal's true nature until it was almost too late. *I couldn't live with myself if I saw warnings Auntie P. didn't and failed to speak up.*

"Just say a prayer I know the right thing to do. Chaz doesn't strike me as the kind of man to take what Hank's done lying down. Pauline's about to launch herself right into a long, angry war between those two brothers."

"I know you love Auntie P., but I'm still not so sure you should stick your nose into this."

Yvonne stared at the swirl of chocolate and caramel in her sundae glass. There was one part of the Neal story she could share at the moment. "Here's the thing. Auntie P. told me she'd had misgivings about Neal. She wasn't sure it was her place to say, and she couldn't be sure about what she felt."

"Okay," Jean replied, "but what's that got to do with this?"

"She told me keeping quiet about Neal was one of her biggest regrets. She asked my forgiveness that she hadn't raised her concerns when she saw them."

Jean pushed out a breath. "So now you don't feel you should stay silent about the concerns you see."

"How can I? I mean, if things went really bad, how could I ever live with myself?"

Jean pursed her lips, thinking. "What if Pauline resents you for interfering?"

"She might. But if I do it right, maybe we'll all be glad I did in the end."

"Maybe." Jean didn't seem convinced, which didn't help Yvonne's confidence. "It'd take just the right words."

"Which is why I'll need loads of prayer. I'm supposed to see both of them in a bit. They're meeting with Pastor Mitchell before he starts the rehearsal for tomorrow's wedding. I'm going to be running around all day tomorrow getting everything ready.

Jean, if I'm going to say anything, it has to be now."

Jean gave a helpless smile. "Well, I suppose it won't be the first time we've faced a challenge with prayer and ice cream."

He was going to be late for church. Well, not in the walk-in-after-service-starts way, but Chaz never liked to be late for anything, much less whatever was happening at Matrimony Valley Community Church in four minutes.

Chaz had walked Cecil three times around the cabin—a slow process given the poor fellow's limp. He was pretty sure Cecil was housebroken but wanted to be sure. In the end he'd left a towel by the door and hoped for the best, leaving a phone message for Kelly or her girls to let Cecil out if they arrived back at the house before he did.

He sprinted down the street, taking the steps in front of the church in two strides. He banged the door open harder than was

needed, sending an echoing boom through the empty sanctuary as if he were an invading warlord. It wasn't that far from how he felt.

Pauline startled a bit. Dad just shot him a look. The person who looked most uncomfortable, however, was Yvonne. She was pacing and looked as if she'd crawl out of her skin any minute. She was bothered about something.

"Sorry I haven't had a chance to meet you yet, Chaz," Pastor Mitchell said, walking up the aisle to greet him. "Welcome to Matrimony Valley." He gestured toward the pew where Pauline and Hank sat. "Your father sure knows how to pick 'em."

They walked down toward the front of the church. "Now, I understand you'll be standing up for your dad."

They hadn't ever discussed it. This whole thing came at such a breakneck speed they'd hardly talked about any of the details. "I am?"

The reverend widened his eyes. "Isn't that why you're here?"

"Between you and me, Pastor, I'm not at all sure why I'm here." He directed those last words straight at Dad.

"Of course you're standing up as my best man," Dad said. "We talked about it."

"We did not. And I'd think given recent developments, you'd want Wyatt for that job."

Pastor Mitchell looked confused. "Is Wyatt your other son?"

Chaz was not in the mood to sit here and play happy wedding while things were still in shambles between Hank and him. "Maybe the words you want are *real son*."

"Chaz." Pauline put a hand out as if that would melt the ice between him and his father. "Let's all try to…"

"Let the boy get it out, Pauline," Hank said, standing his ground in the church aisle. "It don't bother me."

It didn't bother him? Chaz still couldn't

get his mind around his father's seeming indifference to the whole situation.

Chaz turned on his heels, making to leave the sanctuary, when Pauline stood up.

"Well, it bothers me," she announced.

The declaration earned a look from Dad Chaz could never recall seeing on the man's face before.

The air in the pretty little church went thick. Pauline gripped the pew in front of her. Yvonne sank into a pew and looked up at the rafters. Pastor Mitchell's glance bounced among all four of them. Chaz glared at Dad, who glared right back.

Mitchell finally said, "Do y'all need a minute?"

"No," said Dad, at the same time Yvonne and Pauline said, "Yes."

Pauline looked at Yvonne in surprise.

"Nothing more to be said on that subject," Hank said.

"I'm not so sure," came Yvonne's careful reply. "Auntie P., let's you and I take a walk."

"Take a few minutes, Pauline," Pastor Mitchell offered.

Dad scratched his chin as he watched Yvonne pull Pauline from the sanctuary. The minute the door shut, Dad turned on Chaz. "What'd you say to her?"

Chaz spread his hands in frustration. "How should I know? I don't even know which *her* you mean."

Dad pointed to the exit where Pauline and Yvonne had just left. "Those two look like they're about to get into it, and I want to know over what."

"Let's remember that weddings can make everyone tense," Pastor Mitchell said in a very pastorly voice.

Without a single glance in his father's direction, Chaz knew Hank was giving the reverend the exact same look he was giving the man. "I don't know anything. I don't even know why I'm best man."

"Because you're my son," Dad replied, looking a bit hurt for the first time in this whole mess. "Because I wanted to make certain you know you're still a big part of my life. Despite what you may think at the moment."

Chaz tried not to let his chin hit the ground. "You seriously think you can leave Wander Canyon Ranch to Wyatt and it'll all be okay if I get to stand up at your wedding?" Dad used to be one of the most sensible guys he knew. Now it was like aliens had abducted Dad and left some strange impulsive man in his place.

"I think your father was..." Pastor Mitchell began.

"*Step*father." Chaz cut him off, not caring how the correction registered in Hank's eyes.

"...trying to make a meaningful gesture," the pastor continued emphatically, holding his hands between them as if he and

Dad might come to blows right there in the sanctuary.

"Oh, he's made a meaningful gesture all right," Chaz said. "I heard the meaning loud and clear."

"You're taking this all wrong," Dad said. "I'm putting my faith in you to be the bigger man here."

"Well, maybe your faith is misplaced," Chaz shot back. "No offense, Pastor, but I'm not really feeling like much of a stand-up guy at the moment." He stepped out of the pew and started back up the aisle. "I think I'm done here."

To his surprise, Mitchell came after him. "I doubt you are."

When Chaz raised an eyebrow at him, the pastor said, "You two are going to have to talk this out. Starting now seems as good a time as any." He looked back toward Dad. "Hank, are you willing?"

"I suppose." Dad looked anything but, but he sat down in the nearest pew.

Pastor Mitchell stood in front of Chaz, blocking his way to the door. "I don't see how it will help anything," Chaz said.

"Try me," the pastor said, motioning to the pew behind his father. "Arguing in church often turns out better than you think." He sat down opposite Chaz and his father. "Now, let's take a breath here. Let me see if I understand the situation. Hank, you told Chaz last night…"

The back door of the sanctuary pushed open again, cutting off the pastor's words. Pauline marched up the aisle with Yvonne nowhere in sight. She stopped in front of Hank, hands on her hips.

"Well, now you've gone and done it," she declared.

Dad straightened up. "Done what?"

"My niece just informed me she thinks it's a bad idea I marry into this giant argument you call a family." Pauline's voice pitched higher with the threat of tears. "Yvonne just stood out there on the steps and told me she wouldn't be able to forgive herself if she didn't let me know she thinks I might be making a huge mistake in marrying you."

Dad stared at Pauline. "And what do you think?"

To Chaz's surprise, Pauline blinked away tears and said, "Right now I don't know what I think."

"Pauline, honey…" Dad rose off the pew.

"Don't you 'Pauline, honey' me right now. I've tried to stand by you in this, but when my favorite niece thinks you're too cruel to have my heart…"

Dad wasn't cruel. He was just wrong, letting his need to run away from the ranch and go play newlywed interfere with the right way to hand down the ranch.

Pauline's eyes darted back and forth between Chaz and his dad. "My own dear niece felt she couldn't stay silent. She was sobbing, saying she couldn't live with herself if she didn't warn me. About you.

Think about that, Hank. Think about what that says."

The thought of Yvonne sobbing drove Chaz nuts. She didn't deserve to get caught up in the middle of this. Was the engagement going to pile pain on everyone?

# *Chapter Nine*

Flour was everywhere.

Yvonne shouldn't have sent Cathy home so she could be alone in the shop. She should have thought through what to do after she made Auntie P. cry.

She should have known better than to try to balance a huge bag of flour on the edge of the counter, but she was sad and angry and there was so much to be done for tomorrow's wedding.

She turned too quickly with eyes blurred from tears and knocked the enormous bag of flour off the counter. It tumbled down to split open and coat the shop like a powdery bomb. The floor was covered, and the display cases were dusted. Even her hands were white from trying to grab the bag as it fell. She'd just set her time frame for tomorrow's wedding back an hour, if not two.

Then *he* walked in.

The last thing on earth she wanted to see right now was the surprised face of Chaz Walker, taking in her tearstained, flour-covered self standing in the center of her own personal bakery blizzard.

He was trying not to laugh; she could at least give him that much. His face contorted with the effort, eyes taking on that rare amused glint she'd seen only a few times. In her horror, she tried to cover her eyes, realizing too late that her hands were coated in the white stuff, which meant her cheeks now were, as well. "Oh, great," she spit out, disgusted to find that flour coated her lips, as well. "If you get out your cell phone, so help me…"

That sent Chaz over the edge. He burst

out laughing, running his hands down his face. "I didn't even think of that."

"To your credit," she replied, a small cloud puffing up as she grabbed a towel from the counter and wiped her face.

"Didn't help," he managed between more stifled laughs.

She turned to see her reflection in the display case glass and gasped. The streaks of her tear-smudged eye makeup clashed with bands of white dust to make her look like a mime gone horribly wrong. Her shirt bore white blotches, as did her hands.

It was, in fact, hideously funny. An absurd exclamation mark on this whole disastrous set of days. Feeling a laugh work its way up from under all the stress, she made a face into the glass, widening her eyes and sticking her tongue out at herself.

And laughed.

She turned and made the same face at him, just because at the moment it was exactly how she felt. A startled shock replaced the angry sadness when he paused for just a split second before making the same face right back. After all, didn't he have the right to feel the same way given recent events?

They stood there, sticking their tongues out at each other like kindergartners, then laughed louder. It felt like some dam had finally cracked and let loose all the pent-up stress of the wedding, the van, the dinner, the arguments, all of it.

Chaz's laugh was the biggest surprise of all. Rich, full and deep, a whole new side of the quiet sour man who'd invaded her life lately. There was something wondrous about the first water that broke free of the ice and came over the falls in the spring, and Chaz's laugh had the same quality. An escape of the very best kind. The crucial return of something forgotten for a while.

"What happened?" he asked when he could catch his breath.

"I told my aunt I don't think she should marry your dad."

That made Chaz pinch the bridge of his nose. "I meant with the flour."

Somehow her assumption made the whole thing that much funnier. "It fell off the counter. I was sort of in a hurry for tomorrow. And peeved. And sad. When Auntie P. started to cry…"

He scratched his chin. "You expected Pauline to be okay with you saying that?"

"Well, she didn't seem to let it get to her when *you* said it." She picked up the split flour bag only to have it rip farther and deposit a little mountain of white on the floor.

"I'm not her favorite niece."

Yvonne crumpled the now-useless bag. "Well, right now neither am I."

Chaz looked at her for a moment, then reached out his long arm to pick up the garbage can from beside the wall and a cardboard cupcake flavor list. He bent down and deftly slid the paper under the mountain she'd just created, then lifted it to tilt the mass of white powder into the can. A cloud of flour puffed up from the fall, making both of them cough. Was he going to help her clean up?

He was. He used the paper to pick up two more mounds of flour before asking, "Where's your broom?"

There, in those words, was the steady, solid man she'd tried not to admire at the crash site. His offer to help—even in this situation—sank deep under her skin. Chaz Walker was a good man. Gruff? Surely. Stubborn? Absolutely. But a quiet, deep-down good man. She turned back toward the work kitchen. "I'll get it."

He handed her the paper and the garbage can. "You stay put. You'll send up smoke signals if you move from there."

Yvonne scooped up two more paperfuls of flour by the time he returned with her broom and dustpan. He tossed her a towel she'd heard him dampening. "Before it gets in your eyes," he warned, nodding at the streaks that still must be on her face.

While he swept up the floor, she tilted the trash can up against the display case and used the dustpan hand broom to swipe the mounds of flour from the counter. It kept her facing away from him, which kept her from looking at him and knowing he was looking at her.

"Why are you helping me?" She doubted he would give her the real answer, but asked anyway.

He gave a grunt. "Would you want to be in that church with those two right now?"

Chaz had a fair point. Pauline was a gracious woman with a long fuse, but heaven help whoever got to the end of that fuse. She could just imagine the time Pastor Mitchell was having trying to keep the peace between Pauline and Hank.

They worked in silence for a minute or two before he said, "So can I ask you something?"

"Sure. After all, you're sweeping my store."

"Was he like Dad?"

She stopped her cleaning, turning toward him. "Was who like Hank?"

"Whoever you were engaged to. The guy you said was a lot like me. People always say how much Dad and I are alike—given how we're not related and all—and I figure if he was like Hank that might be why you don't like him."

Yvonne leaned back against the case. "For starters, I don't not like him. I thought he was great for Auntie P....well, before now. I don't like what he did to you and Wyatt."

"Yeah, well, that makes two of us."

Yvonne's brain snagged on the way he said "two of us." They weren't any kind of team—except maybe on the current state of her bakery. And tomorrow's deliveries, if he was still showing up. Her wanting him to help had little to do with the tight time crunch of tomorrow's bakery deliveries or how every conversation she had with him seemed to end in an argument.

"What he did doesn't seem like a man

who understands how a family is supposed to work." She hesitated just a bit before adding, "I'm not so sure I want her joining a family like that."

"A family like mine, you mean." His words could have been a challenge, but they were more like an assessment. Did he see his family in the same broken light she did? How could he not after what had happened? "And you still haven't answered my question."

Was Neal like Hank? She'd never really thought about how the two compared before now. "Stubborn," she offered, without further explanation. "Sure he was right, even when he was dead wrong."

"That's what you think of me, then." He'd drawn the connection even if she hadn't.

Yvonne opted for honesty. "At the moment I don't know what I think."

He went back to sweeping. "Funny, that's what your aunt just said. Why are they in such a hurry? To marry, I mean. Do you know?" He punctuated his words with short, irritated broom strokes. "He's never been in a hurry to do anything before this. Now he's in a hurry to do everything."

She offered the words Pauline had given her. "Auntie P. says it's not hard to know exactly what you want when you aren't sure how many years you have left."

"I know exactly what I want," he grumbled as he dumped another mound of flour into the can.

*I don't.* She'd been trying to figure it out since the restlessness had come over her this summer, but she hadn't succeeded. Last year a thriving bakery in Matrimony Valley was her definition of success. This valley had been her home all her life, which didn't explain why it felt small and tight lately. Like the mountains were creeping in on her. She continued cleaning in silence, grateful for his assistance but unsettled by his questions, until he launched another.

"What'd he do?"

"Who?"

"The guy you broke it off with. Someone as crazy about weddings as you, well, he'd have to do something pretty nasty, seems to me."

Now, here was some dangerous ground. "What did Neal do? That I ended it?"

"Yeah."

This was the last story she wanted to tell Chaz Walker, but there didn't seem an easy way out of it. And somehow, after what she'd just said to Auntie P., she needed to spit it out. "Oddly enough, it started with a car accident."

"Get into a lot of those, do you?"

She shot him a look. "*His* car. East of town. And a dog."

Chaz stopped sweeping. He didn't speak, just stood there waiting for her to continue.

"He was driving back from a late appointment in Greenville, and he told me he hit a dog that wandered onto the road. Not too different from last night, I suppose."

"Did the dog survive?"

"He couldn't be bothered to check. We got into an argument about it." It was amazing how the old knot of ice could rise up when she thought about that night.

"You broke off your engagement because your fiancé hit a dog?"

Yvonne looked Chaz straight in the eye. "No. I broke off the engagement because he hit me when I called him on it."

*He hit me.* The air in the bakery seemed to change with her admission. There were things in life Chaz had absolutely no tolerance for, and a man striking a woman—any man striking any woman, no matter what the circumstances—was one of them. The thought of anyone raising a hand to the tiny, feisty, bubbling woman in front of him churned up a burning in his gut.

Yvonne seemed to sense his reaction. "Only once, but that's all it takes, as far as

I'm concerned. I loved him—or thought I did—but it was over from that moment."

What were you supposed to say to something like that? "Rough," he said, unable to come up with something more.

She scrubbed at a spot on the display case. "Yes, it was. He was from around here, so I chose not to tell people what had happened. I told him to leave town after that. Most people probably think it was because I broke his heart, but I made it a condition of my silence." She stopped wiping and met his gaze. "That wasn't a smart bargain to strike, and I've always regretted that decision. So maybe you can see why I take to speaking my mind these days."

She didn't think...? He stepped over to where she was standing. "Dad may be a lot of things, but he would never, ever lay a hand on Pauline."

"No, he doesn't strike me as that kind." Her chin rose, still faintly streaked in white as it was. "But cruelty comes in lots of different flavors, doesn't it?"

He'd thought her reaction to the dog incident was a bit extreme, but now it was easy to see how that night had touched on old wounds. It explained how she took to Cecil and was so invested in the dog's survival. It explained why she was so willing to help him take care of a strange dog in the middle of the night. It didn't explain how drawn he was to her, but nothing explained that, did it?

"No matter what he chose to do to me, I doubt he'd choose to hurt Pauline. I think they genuinely love each other." The words felt goofy coming out of his mouth.

"Not always enough, though, is it?" The sharp chill that overtook her features told him it certainly hadn't been enough for her. How could any decent man do something like that to her?

He looked back over at the little white church. Hank and Pauline were supposed to be going to the wedding of a friend of Pauline's there tomorrow. Would they still go? Or would he and Dad be getting on a plane back to Colorado tomorrow?

"What do you think will happen?" He certainly didn't have a clue.

She blinked several times, the ice in her eyes turning to welling tears. "I think I might be about to bake my last wedding cake for a while."

The pain in her voice sent a jab through his ribs. He went back to his broom rather than meet her eyes and let the jab go deeper. It didn't work—he could still hear her sniffling. Chaz squinted his eyes shut in anguish. Why had he let himself get pulled into this mess of a trip?

He was getting ready to walk over to her and say something uncharacteristically supportive when he was saved by the bell above the bakery door.

"Whoa," Kelly the florist said as she took in the white film that still coated the room. "I thought we already had a blizzard this year."

Yvonne straightened and threw on a happy face. "Very funny."

"You okay? I heard what happened. Actually, I sort of walked in on what happened."

"Pauline and Hank still going at it?" Chaz asked.

Kelly turned to him. "Yes, but I think Pastor Mitchell might have it under control. He said you'd be here." Her glance bounced between Chaz and Yvonne. "He also said to tread carefully, that I might be walking into an argument as big as the one I just left." She looked at Yvonne again. "You okay?" she repeated.

"Things just got a bit out of hand," Yvonne replied.

"You should head over there in a bit, Chaz." Kelly walked farther into the room, carefully avoiding the splotches of flour still scattered across the floor. "But I came to find you first. To give you fair warning."

"That my dad's in the middle of a row with Pauline? Knew that already."

Kelly tucked her hair behind her ear. "Well, that, too, now. But I was coming over first to tell you that Lulu and Carly are going to ask you if they can put Cecil in the church pet parade on Sunday. If you're still here, that is. You're not…leaving, are you?"

Yvonne's hand went to her mouth, stifling a laugh. "The pet parade. Oh, I should have seen that coming, with Cecil romping around the girls' backyard and them having no dog of their own."

"I have no idea if we're staying or leaving. And what in the world is a pet parade?" Whether or not Pauline and Dad patched things up enough to go to tomorrow's wedding, the high fee to change his return flight to Colorado was starting to look worth it.

"Just like it sounds," the florist said. "The church kids parade pets down the avenue. This morning Lulu and Carly decided they want to enter Cecil—if you'd let them."

So now if he wanted to leave he was going to have to deny two little girls the chance to enter his dog in a parade? There was no way to do that without coming off like an ogre. Chaz pinched the bridge of his nose. "Your girls want to walk my dog down the street in a parade?" The strangest sentences he'd ever uttered kept coming out of his mouth since setting foot in Matrimony Valley.

"Well," Yvonne added, barely without laughing, "it's a bit more than that."

He chose his next words carefully. "How much more?"

"They dress him up," Yvonne added. "It's a pet *costume* parade."

## Chapter Ten

She shouldn't laugh. Chaz looked about ready to split open like her flour sack had done. But the thought of his consenting to Cecil's being in the parade was just so funny. Today had been such a ball of pain so far, and it felt so good to laugh again.

"The pet parade is a big deal," she offered, slipping into the cheerful and persuasive tone she often used with stressed brides. "Everybody in town loves it, and it'll take place on Sunday, when we're all done with the wedding. I don't know why I didn't think of putting Cecil in before now."

Actually, Yvonne knew *exactly* why the

prospect of Cecil's entry hadn't dawned on her: there wasn't a Matrimony Valley event less likely to appeal to Chaz Walker. It was silly and fun and lighthearted—everything the man in front of her hadn't shown much capacity to be.

But did he have that side of him hidden somewhere deep down? The thought intrigued her more than she wanted to admit.

Chaz drew his lips together in a tight line. "What kind of costume did the girls have in mind?"

One look at Kelly's face told Yvonne the answer was even worse than she'd suspected. "Well, the girls had a clown in mind, actually."

Chaz actually winced, although he drew a hand down his face in an attempt to hide it. There was a long silence before he looked at Kelly and said, "Your girls want permission to dress my dog up as a circus clown and walk him through the center of town."

It didn't sound anything close to silly and

fun and lighthearted the way he said it. As a matter of fact, he said it as if Kelly just requested he swap out his own jeans and cowboy boots for a tutu and ballerina slippers. With rainbow glitter.

Kelly scrambled to salvage the request. "Actually, given his leg, they're thinking of pulling Cecil in a little red wagon." Kelly reluctantly added, "Decorated like a circus wagon, of course."

"Oh, that'll be adorable," Yvonne coaxed, suddenly eager for something so delightful. "Loads of fun."

Chaz slanted her a doubtful look. "Fun for whom?"

While Yvonne was momentarily impressed by Chaz's correct use of grammar, the unspoken *surely not for me or my dog* came through loud and clear. "Fun for everyone," she replied as if she couldn't see his obvious resistance. "I love the pet parade. It's my favorite fall event. Well, that and the pie contest, which I'm not allowed to enter because, well, I'm a professional and all." She was babbling, but today had taxed her well beyond her composure and Chaz looked a far cry from convinced.

"You won't have to do anything," Kelly appeased. "Just lend Cecil to Carly and Lulu for the parade on Sunday after church. And maybe submit to a few costume fittings. For him, of course," she hastened to add. "Not you."

The thought of Chaz submitting to little-girl costume fittings made Yvonne burst out in an unhelpful yelp of laughter. She took a deep breath rather than clap her hand over her mouth again. "Think of it as a completely painless way to make two little girls deliriously happy. After all, Carly and Lulu are sweethearts, and you said they've been helpful with Cecil."

When Chaz offered no reply—or indication that he was inclined to agree to this charade—Yvonne pressed on. "I'd let them have my dog—if I had one."

"Please?" Kelly's single word was filled with a loving mom's reluctance to disappoint her little girls.

In a surge of inspiration, Yvonne added in a loud whisper, "No one in Wander Canyon ever has to know."

That teasing produced the tiniest crack in Chaz's expression. "Why do I feel outnumbered here?"

"Four females against a man and his dog? You are." Challenging as it was, Yvonne found she enjoyed trying to bring his lighter side out. Chaz didn't answer right away, leaving Kelly and Yvonne to trade hopeful looks. Yvonne sent up a prayer. *Come on, Lord, work a little wonder here. There's been too much pain to go around lately.*

Chaz stuffed one hand in his pocket. "I'm sure I'll regret this..."

Not a resounding agreement, but Kelly was smart enough to run with what she got before Chaz could change his mind. "Thanks so much. The girls will be thrilled.

And it will be fun, I promise." She turned toward the door. "Hope things work out over there at the church. We all love Pauline and want her to be happy." With that, the florist was out the door.

Yvonne waved goodbye to her friend, feeling Chaz's eyes on her the whole time. She turned back to him. "That was a nice thing to do."

He almost smiled at her—almost. "You all are just plain crazy here—you know that?"

She smiled herself as she picked the rag back up and resumed wiping down the counter. Her small inner spark of happy victory glowed against all the tension and strain. "Lots of towns have pet parades. And first prize is fifty dollars. Split three ways that could buy you a whole bag of kibble. Or I could give you a really sweet deal on cookies."

"They're going to dress up my dog." His

*how did that just happen?* look was all too endearing.

She simply smiled wider and said, "Yes, they are."

Chaz looked out the window at Kelly making her way back across the street. "I suppose the fact that I hate clowns matters about as much as the fact that my dad hates chocolate."

Yvonne laughed and set the rag down again. "Chaz Walker, is there anything you *do* like?"

He surprised her by answering. "A good steak."

He didn't stop there. A list came tumbling out of him in one long startling stream, each item punctuated by a point of his finger. "And strong, hot coffee. A well-built fence. A good horse. Comfortable jeans. My boots. Really cold root beer." He looked her straight in the eye for a long moment before finishing with, "And feeling like someone actually gives a hoot what I think."

* * *

After leaving the bakery, Chaz had no intention of going back into that church. It wouldn't do anyone much good to get a conversation out of Hank Walker before he was ready. Dad knew where to find him if he wanted to talk. Still, Chaz decided to at least make the gesture of leaving a message at the inn. If things had settled down, someone would tell him soon enough.

He chose instead to pass the afternoon sitting on the front steps of the cabin, brushing the last of the mats out of Cecil's hair. He liked this dog. More than he could explain. In fact, it made him crazy to think of someone abandoning the poor fellow out in the North Carolina forest like that.

Chaz had always considered ownership of an animal a sort of moral obligation. You did right by the animals under your care, always. It was an essential value to how he ran the ranch. Wyatt, on the other hand, was always digging up shortcuts or launching off in new scheming directions. Chaz did his best to ignore what he could and improve upon what he couldn't.

He mostly kept a steady focus, worked hard and made sure the herd never got too large to be properly fed and cared for. Technically, as manager he could still ensure that happened, but the fact that Wyatt would now have final say as owner stuck in his craw. How was he ever going to make peace with Dad's decision? Was it even possible?

Cecil winced as Chaz's frustration made him yank on the brush too hard as he worked a tangle out of the shepherd mix's tail. "Sorry about that," he consoled the animal. "You've got way too many mats—it's either this or shave you, and from what I hear, Sunday will be embarrassing enough without you looking like a shorn sheep. Trust me, I'll keep those mats from ever happening again."

As if he heard the promise, Cecil looked up at Chaz with his soulful eyes. He shifted around to face Chaz, his bandaged leg thumping on the porch wood beneath him. Chaz ran his hands over the cast, making sure it wasn't too tight. "Hurts less today, I hope."

The echo of Lulu's and Carly's laughter came from the open kitchen window across the yard. He tried to imagine Cecil being wheeled down Aisle Avenue in a wagon, sure whatever costume he could dream up wouldn't be half as crazy as what those two girls had in mind. "Sorry I sold you down the river on that one." He sighed long and hard as he ran a hand over the dog's black-and-tan coat. "We've all been sold down the river these days."

He looked up to see Yvonne walking up the driveway alongside Kelly's house. At first he thought she was heading into Kelly's side door, but the look on her face and the direction of her steps told him she was headed straight for him.

She must have come from talking to Pauline. Her expression told him she didn't bring happy news.

Stopping in front of him, she folded her hands in front of her. "They called off the wedding. Did Hank tell you?"

"I haven't talked to Dad. I thought it best to give him a little space right now. But I figured that might be how it ended up."

Yvonne gave a wobbly sigh and sank down on one of the two brightly colored Adirondack chairs in the cabin's front yard. Cecil hobbled over to say hello, dropping his head into Yvonne's lap. She offered the dog a damp smile and scratched Cecil behind the ears.

"It's what you wanted, isn't it?" Even as he said the words, it struck him that he'd agreed to come on this trip half to achieve just that—to put the brakes on this rush of a wedding. Now that it had happened, now that he had surprised himself by coming around about Pauline, he didn't know what to think. *You can't rush things like this—it never turns out*, he reminded himself. Marriage was supposed to be a lifelong thing, not a spur-of-the-moment impulse. Was it any wonder the whole escapade was starting to feel like a giant mistake?

"Yes," Yvonne answered his question, then quickly added, "and no. Certainly not like this. Not because of something I said." Yvonne let her head fall back against the chair. "Will you stay?"

Chaz realized that if he and Dad left now, Yvonne would blame herself for the girls' losing out on the pet parade, as well. He'd have to stay. He couldn't add to the pile of guilt he already saw pressing down on Yvonne's shoulders. And, if he was honest, part of him truly wanted to help her with tomorrow's delivery. After all, that wedding was going on even if Hank and Pauline's wasn't. It wasn't that hard to say, "I think so."

"You don't have to." Despite her words, Chaz could easily see she'd much rather he stay. Was it only for logistical reasons? Or was the baffling pull he felt toward her growing on her side, as well?

He stuck with the safer logistical case. "I promised my dog to those girls and to help you with deliveries tomorrow. I keep my word." He wanted to add "unlike Dad," but he'd realized in the middle of the night last night that Dad had never come out and promised Wander would go to him. Just made him feel like it, like an equal son, like a Walker who would inherit Walker land.

"I broke up Hank and Auntie P. I had to open my big mouth and meddle. The last thing I ever wanted to do in this world is break an engagement. Not after having lived through it with Neal."

How on earth could she feel bad about breaking an engagement with this Neal jerk? And for the reasons she had? Then again, even justified pain was still pain. He'd had to put a favorite horse down last year, and even though he knew it was the right thing to do, it hollowed his heart out for days. He had to admire how she could whip up cake after cake for other people's happiness after being hurt like that.

"Who's got the ring?" He'd tried to hide his shock the day Dad showed him the ring he'd bought in Denver and announced his intention to propose. It was a big ring. Flashy. Something else out of character for Dad.

Yvonne cocked her head, eyes narrowing as she remembered. "Now that I think about it, it's still on her finger."

That seemed important. "Do you know for a fact that it's off? What if they just did something sensible, like hit the pause button." Wait…was he now actually pulling for them as a couple? He was, *if* they could manage to be sensible about things. And he wasn't sure that was possible yet. "Your aunt strikes me as the kind to take that ring off and throw it in the river—if not in Dad's face—if she was really done with him."

She managed a small laugh. "Like Ziggy's lug nuts?"

He liked that he made her laugh. "I guess." He set down the dog brush and came to sit in the chair next to her. "Is she mad at you? For coming out and saying what you did?" Yvonne had been brave for saying something bound to hurt her aunt like that. Not too many people in this world were willing to love hard like that when it might cost them so much.

"I'm not sure. Hurt, for sure. Sad, some. But she can't really be mad at me."

She'd looked mad enough when she'd come stomping back into the sanctuary. And Dad had certainly hauled off at him when Chaz had ventured to voice his own reservations about the marriage. "Why not?"

Yvonne tilted her head to look at him. She was close enough that he could see the different colors in her hair and a faint splash of freckles on her cheeks. "Because Pauline had been against my marrying Neal from the beginning and never said so. She's one of only a few people who know the real reason I broke it off with Neal. When I did tell her, she told me she would always regret not telling me how she felt earlier."

That explained some of the wounds he saw in her. And explained why Yvonne felt suddenly compelled to stick her nose into Dad and Pauline's business. She was fiercely loyal—he could see that in her same as in himself—and there wasn't a deeper slice you could make into a loyal person than to betray them. Wasn't that exactly what he was living now?

"So…maybe this pause in the wedding planning is a good thing. Well," he amended when she really rolled her eyes at that remark, "a not-terrible thing."

She leaned toward him, and he smelled cinnamon and vanilla and a bunch of other baking scents on her. "Is that how you feel right now? Tell me, do you feel anything even close to 'not terrible'?"

Actually, he did. Inexplicably, his mood had improved since the blowup in the church. No, that wasn't true, either. His mood had lightened even before that. It had brightened at taking Cecil in. And then again at the riverbank throwing those absurd lug nuts in the river. And again in the bakery. All times Yvonne was with him. The woman was annoying, contradictory and meddling, but she somehow gave him a lightness that made no sense.

Thoughts like that banging around in his head made her feel too close. Chaz picked up a dog toy he'd bought from the hardware store and waved it to get Cecil's attention. Playing fetch was out of the question, but a low-key bit of tug-of-war was possible. He was grateful when Cecil lumbered over to where they were sitting and began pulling on the toy.

"How's Hank taking it?" Yvonne asked.

"Like I said, I don't know. He's not the kind of man you go hounding with questions when he's angry."

"So you're not going to talk to him? You're just going to leave him alone?"

He looked up at her. "Not everyone feels like they have to meddle in everything all the time." Cecil tugged on the toy again. "I have no doubt he'll come find me and give me a piece of his mind when he's ready."

"Well, how do you think he is? If you had to guess."

He resisted the urge to answer "I don't care" and instead said, "Ticked off. Surprised. I don't think he expected this to end with Pauline calling it off. Or postponing." He was never against their marrying, just doing it so as quickly as they'd been planning.

Yvonne sank back into the chair. She pulled in a deep breath and waved her hands in front of her face the way women did when they were trying not to cry. "I was thinking this might have been my grand finale in the valley. Now it'll just be the wedding I ruined."

He thought Hank had ruined it all on his own, but her other choice of words was telling. "Finale?"

She widened her eyes and pulled her knees up to hug them. She clearly hadn't intended that slip. "I didn't mean to say it like that."

Was there more to her desire to go all out on this wedding than just affection for her aunt? He leaned slightly in her direction. "Are you thinking about leaving here?"

With a look back at the house, Yvonne leaned in within inches of his shoulder. "Don't ask me that."

He didn't know how to process the fact that he could read her so clearly. "You are. You're thinking about leaving Matrimony Valley." He said it softly because they were so close, but with enough force to let her know he wouldn't let her evade the issue.

Her gaze fell to the chair's wide arms, and she ran her finger down a crack in the wood. "Maybe."

That surprised him. "I thought you loved it here."

"I do. Well, I did. I just... I don't know. I've just got this craving for a fresh start. Someplace new, bigger, where I'm someone other than the cake lady down the street."

He understood the craving to make something of yourself. To know you were capable of more than what most people thought.

"I was going to go all out for Pauline and Hank's wedding, you know?" she went on. "Maybe I should have just kept my mouth shut."

"No," he shot back, with enough force that she pulled a bit away. He softened his tone again and ignored the foolish urge to touch her arm. "You don't keep your mouth shut about things like that. Ever." He paused for a moment before adding, "You may have spurred Pauline on, but seems to me no one makes that woman do anything she doesn't have a mind to."

"So what do we do now?"

His brain ran off in startling directions on that question. There were a hundred reasons why the irrational, unexpected hum of attraction he was coming to feel for her was a bad idea. All this was about Hank and Pauline, and certainly not about him and Yvonne. "We let them work it out between themselves. This isn't anything we can fix for them. So *we* don't do anything."

She opened her mouth to reply, then clapped it shut again. She rose up off the chair, dusted herself off and headed back down the driveway.

The lightness in him seemed to leave in her wake. So he offered the only consolation that came to mind. "Well, Cecil, for once I actually got the last word with that woman."

The only trouble was, those words were "We don't do anything."

## Chapter Eleven

With her usual assistant, Cathy, headed out of town for a family event, Yvonne was doubly grateful when Chaz knocked on the bakery door at nine forty-five the next morning. "What a pleasant surprise to meet a dependable man." Life hadn't shown her too many men of that variety, except for the terrific ones who had married her friends Kelly and Jean. And that, as far as she knew, used up Matrimony Valley's supply of decent guys.

Yvonne pointed at the counter as she walked toward the tall bakery racks in the back of the store. "There's coffee there.

And half a dozen oatmeal raisin cookies if you're hungry."

He followed her. "I had something that *looked* like coffee at the cabin, but I prefer yours by far." His compliment pleased her. "And cookies…" After filling a mug, Chaz grabbed a cookie and offered her an actual smile as he tucked a second into his shirt pocket.

"Have you talked to Hank yet?"

He gave a small grunt. "A little. He mostly kept to himself yesterday, like I expected. Turns out Bill Williams at the outfitters took him fishing, which was probably the best thing he could do."

They'd talked about fishing over dinner at the steak house. She got the impression it was something Chaz liked to do with his stepfather. She pulled the first box of sweets down off the shelf and loaded it onto a wheeled cart for transport across the street to Hailey's Inn Love, where the reception was going to be. "You didn't go?"

"Like I said, I thought it best we kept our distance yesterday." He stretched up to fetch the box off the higher shelf, reaching it easily. He was rather tall—well over six feet—but not at all gangly. Rather, he had a precise lean and muscular look to him, a man with no need of excess, one at home in his own skin. "I figured if we spent too long together, we'd end up in an argument, and that seems to be the last thing everybody needs right now." He was trying to hide it, but she could see Chaz's disappointment that his father had gone fishing with someone else—even under these conditions. *There really is a soft heart somewhere under there.*

He slid the box onto the cart, stopping momentarily to offer a masculine frown at the pink-and-purple frosting on the cupcakes. "So I took Cecil for a short walk, then had a long, friendly visit with Rob at the hardware store while Cecil had his first costume fitting."

Yvonne had fun picturing that. "How'd that go?"

He narrowed one eye. "Don't know. Don't wanna know."

"Oh, I'm sure the costume fitting was adorable, but I was talking about Rob." Yvonne handed him a box of pink and purple macarons to add while she retrieved the tiered tray on which they'd sit. Days ago if anyone had told her she'd be enjoying a conversation with Chaz Walker while he helped her deliver pink and purple sweets, she'd never have believed them. "Rob's in the middle of his own whirlwind engagement, you know."

Chaz grimaced at the cookie colors. "Oh, he told me all about it. Samantha this and Samantha that. Suddenly I'm surrounded by love-struck old men."

She chuckled. "Samantha was in the valley to cover an unusual wedding for *Southeastern Nuptials* magazine when a huge snowstorm hit. She slipped on the ice outside Rob's hardware store." She grinned. "I suppose you could say she really fell for him."

Chaz gave a dramatic groan as they began to push the cart toward the front door. Since the wedding was only across the street, it was just a matter of ferrying items back and forth on a wheeled cart. "Do you have a whole supply of bad wedding jokes like that?"

"Maybe a small collection. Anyway, Rob has always been a nice guy, but some whole new side of him came out with Samantha as he took care of her. She'd been kind of a grump during her visit up until then, and I kid you not, it was like she just melted in front of him." She indulged in a romantic sigh. "It was the strangest, happiest case of love at first sight I've ever seen."

He stopped pushing the cart for a moment. "You believe in that sort of thing?"

"Of course I do. I've seen it. You've seen

it." His resulting expression led her to say, "Clearly, you don't believe in it."

"Infatuation at first sight, maybe. Not love."

She pushed the front door of the shop open as he wheeled the cart through. "Mind the curb there."

Chaz simply picked up the entire cart, carried it over the curb and set it down on the street as if he were toting a bag of groceries. Big, strapping cowboy delivery help had its advantages.

"I admit, I still have a hard time swallowing Dad's instant declaration of true love. I don't think it can happen that fast and be…well, true. Dad thought we'd both be thrilled, and was a bit ticked off when I wasn't."

That was telling. "But Wyatt was?" As they made their way across the street, Yvonne wondered why Wyatt wasn't here instead of—or in addition to—Chaz. Hank's actions were beyond puzzling to her.

"Oh, Wyatt thought it was great, but Wyatt falls for a different woman every week."

The disapproval in his voice made her ask, "Have you ever been in love?"

That was probably too personal a question for someone like him. But surprisingly, he answered. "I've never been as smitten as Dad, no."

"But you have been in love."

"I thought I was in love once. In college." Something passed across his eyes.

"What happened?"

He paused for a moment, as if deciding what to say, then began pushing the cart again. "Let's just say I discovered she didn't share my opinion."

She leaned over the cart. "She cheated on you?"

He shook his head. "Nothing that dramatic. It was more like I didn't...couldn't... hold much interest for her." He clearly decided to change the subject when he asked, "Have you talked to Pauline?"

She began guiding the cart toward the side door of Hailey's Inn Love. "We had a long conversation last night. She's going to the wedding alone today. She's taking this hard."

"She thinks what Dad did was wrong. She told me so herself, that she hoped to change his mind. I wanted her to change his mind." He hoisted the cart up over the opposite curb as easily as he had on the bakery side of the street. He carried his large frame with such an ease that she hadn't realized how physically strong he must have to be for his line of work. "Maybe Pauline woke up to the fact that he's not the kind of man to change his mind about anything."

Bitterness cut sharp edges into his words. The ranch succession wedged a gap between father and son that might not ever heal. Still, was this more of an issue between father and son than between bride and groom? Had she done the right thing in airing her doubts?

"I get that," she answered Chaz, "but it still feels off. I expected Auntie P. to push back, to convince me I was wrong. Instead, she called everything off. That's not like her. She's normally a 'let's work it through' kind of person."

Down the street, three women in pink-and-lavender dresses were heading up the church steps for the church ceremony. Yvonne waved to Kelly, who was just behind the bridal party with a box of bouquets and boutonnieres. The happy procession stung just a little, knowing Pauline and Hank might not get their day.

"But you said she didn't give back the ring. Maybe she didn't call it off completely."

"That's what I can't work out. She's talking like everything's off, but she still has the ring on her finger. I can't make sense of it."

Chaz gave a sour laugh. "None of this stuff makes any sense at all, if you ask me."

They pushed through the delivery door and Yvonne pointed Chaz across the lobby in the direction of the inn's ballroom. She pulled the cart to a stop, however, when Hank Walker appeared over Chaz's shoulder.

Hank was clearly not dressed to attend the wedding. As a matter of fact, he looked awful. "Morning," he mumbled, and then he shrugged. "Not going to the wedding."

"I can see that," Chaz commented.

It was supposed to have been Hank's unofficial introduction to the family. Now the whole day would have this sad, awkward taint to it. Yvonne was glad she had bakery tasks to hide behind. Yvonne could just imagine what Mama and her sisters would say if they knew she'd been the one to meddle in Hank and Pauline's plans. Would Pauline tell them?

Chaz began maneuvering the cart around

Hank. Hank let him pass but put his hand out to stop Yvonne. "Can you spare a minute? I mean, after you get things set up and all."

Hank wanted to talk to her? Or did he want to give her a piece of his mind for interfering?

Chaz sent a suspicious look toward Hank but then simply said, "I'll take these in there," and started pulling the cart toward the reception room. "Come in when you're done with him." Yvonne stared after Chaz as he lumbered down the hall pulling the cart of baked goods before turning in curiosity to the man beside her.

Hank looked more sad than angry, which she hoped meant he didn't blame her for what had happened. There seemed no good way out of the whole situation. Her father's words to her after she broke it off with Neal came back from her memory. "When someone shows you their true self, don't blame them, believe them." She believed Hank's actions showed his true self and had acted on that belief. She didn't relish the prospect of having to defend that in the middle of setting up for a wedding.

Hank caught her discomfort and shifted his weight. "I won't take up much of your time. I know we're not on good terms at the moment. So I realize what I'm going to ask is going to seem strange. Just think on what I'm about to say, okay?"

Yvonne turned to face him fully, telling herself to listen to whatever strange request this man seemed ready to make. "Okay."

"I want you to come to Wander Canyon."

She felt her jaw drop. "What?"

*What in the world could Dad have to say to Yvonne? Especially now?* Chaz practically mumbled the questions out loud as he pushed open the doors to the inn's large reception room. His brain concocted dozens of possibilities—none of them very good—as he maneuvered the cart full of baked goods through a maze of round tables set up for the reception.

Finally, he parked the cart next to the long table at the far side of the room Yvonne had told him would serve as the event's dessert table. The sheer fact that he knew what a dessert table was, where it was in this particular room and that he had just squired a cart of cupcakes and cookies toward it bugged him endlessly.

He looked back toward the closed doors. Part of him wanted to defy Dad's expression and stay there with Yvonne. He didn't take to the idea of Dad dressing her down for meddling, especially in the middle of an inn lobby. He also suspected Yvonne could hold her own, even against Dad. And truth be told, he didn't want to be in any room with his father right now.

He deposited the boxes onto the table, then just stood there for a second, looking around. An awkward, out-of-place sensation overtook him in the empty room filled with pink and purple decorations. How had he been yanked out of his life in Colorado to be here, doing this?

Hands planted in defiance on his hips, Chaz looked back toward the door again. *Only take a minute, huh, Dad?* Curiosity vied with anxiety that Yvonne hadn't yet returned. Dad was talking to Yvonne. What was more, Dad was talking to Yvonne *and not to him*, which only added to the tangled, tumbling sensation that hadn't left him since arriving in Matrimony Valley.

Twice he started toward the door but stopped himself. Go after her? Stand here until she came to him and told him whatever it was Dad had to say?

It was ten whole minutes before Yvonne pushed through the door, looking…well… stunned. Not shocked or hurt—like he'd felt when Dad pronounced his decision—but more like baffled. As if Dad had said something outrageous to her and she didn't quite know what to make of it. Was that better than his yelling at her, or worse?

"Well?" he barked impatiently, then corrected himself and asked, "What did he have to say?" in a more civilized tone.

Yvonne ran one hand across the back of her neck as she walked farther into the room. "I thought he was going to lay into me."

"He didn't?" None of this was Yvonne's fault, and he'd storm out there and make sure Dad knew it if he had to.

"No." She glanced back at the door once, as if she half expected Dad to follow her in here. Then she looked up at him with bewildered eyes. "Chaz, he asked me if I would come back with him to visit Wander Canyon."

He couldn't have heard right. "He what?"

She acknowledged his shock with a shrug and a nod. "He asked me to come back with you and him to visit the ranch in Colorado when you go home on Monday."

"Why?"

"Well, he says I'll better understand why he did what he did and could maybe help convince Pauline to go through with the wedding."

That made no sense whatsoever. "I've lived most of my life on the ranch and *I* don't understand why he did what he did!" Chaz realized he'd raised his voice and clapped his mouth shut. Dad was behaving like a madman. Or a man desperate enough to try anything to win back Pauline. He didn't know which explanation was more disturbing, especially since it was starting to feel as if his own common sense was unraveling.

This move—bizarre as it was—told him one important thing. It confirmed his own theory that Pauline was the only person capable of changing Dad's mind on the succession plan. Dad cared what Pauline thought, cared enough to enlist any ally to bring her back around.

That meant that Pauline—and evidently now Yvonne—might still be his best chance to salvage this succession mess. He could never argue Hank out of his decision, but maybe Pauline could.

"Are you going to go?" he asked. The thought of Yvonne visiting Wander Canyon Ranch created a dual buzz of both pleasure and panic in his chest.

She clasped her hands together. "I don't know. Why would he do that? I mean, I know what he told me, but…why?"

Chaz threw his hands up in the air. "If you're looking at me for an explanation, I'm fresh out."

Yvonne made a small, confused noise, then started walking toward the cart. That was right—they were in the middle of a wedding. He and Yvonne still had a second trip to make.

He started weaving through the tables behind her. "What'd you tell him?"

"I told him I'd think about it."

Chaz stopped walking. "You're seriously considering it?" The buzz in his chest doubled.

"Well, I didn't think I ought to refuse him outright standing there in the lobby. He knows what I think of his actions. It must have cost him quite a bit to make a request like that to me." She looked at Chaz. "I get the impression Walker men have to be pretty hard up to enlist the help of the enemy."

Was she referring to his own surprising alliance with Pauline? Yvonne reached the cart and began pushing it toward the door. Chaz was starting to feel like Cecil, following this baker around like he was on a leash. "Very funny."

This did not sound like Dad at all. Dad mostly *told*. Dad rarely *asked*. Certainly Dad had rarely asked *him*. No, he'd been told the ranch's future was being yanked out from underneath him. Now Dad was asking? Extending olive-branch invitations to Yvonne to come to Wander? "You're not really gonna think about it, are you?"

She pursed her lips. "I don't know."

She really was going to think about it. She might actually take Dad up on the offer. On some level, Chaz could follow his father's thinking, that bringing Yvonne around was the first step in bringing Pauline around. On the other hand, Chaz didn't see where it had any hope of solving anything. In fact, he could think of a dozen ways it could make everything worse.

"You can't just up and go…can you?" Yvonne was the only baker in town. Even if this was the last wedding of the season, could she leave the shop on such short notice?

"As a matter of fact, the timing isn't too bad."

That wasn't the answer he was expecting.

"I've got no van until Ziggy finds me a good deal." She stopped pushing the cart for

204 *Wander Canyon Courtship*

a moment. "And as of yesterday's drama, this is the last wedding of the season for me. Cathy's been saying she wants to learn how to run a bakery. Maybe it's time I let her try running mine for a few days."

Chaz would never hand his business over to someone he wasn't absolutely sure was ready. It was part of the reason this whole mess with Wyatt burned him so—Wyatt wasn't ready. Far from it. Was Yvonne so ready to close this chapter of her life that she'd risk Bliss Bakery?

"Maybe this is one of those perfect coincidences Auntie P. always talks about."

Chaz didn't believe in coincidences. "What are you going to tell Pauline?"

Yvonne resumed pushing the cart through the inn hallway. "I don't know that yet, either. But I don't have to, because right now we've got a wedding to set up. Let's get that cake across the street before too many of the guests are in the lobby."

With that, Yvonne pushed the cart right

out the door and down the street like the world hadn't just tilted off its axis with Dad's crazy invitation.

## *Chapter Twelve*

Two hours later, Yvonne stood next to Pauline at the wedding reception. They'd both put on happy faces for the event, offering good wishes for the bride and groom, but it still felt bittersweet to be admiring the wedding cake.

"This one is beautiful, honey," her aunt said. Her words lacked their usual sparkle. "You always make such beautiful cakes."

Yvonne swallowed back the lump in her throat. It felt wrong for this to be the last cake of the season. That was supposed to belong to Hank and Pauline. This was a lovely cake, but theirs would have been even lovelier.

"I don't blame you, you know," Pauline said after a deep breath. "Your mama and I raised you to speak your mind. And you didn't say anything I wasn't already thinking. You just sort of woke me up to how deep a rift is going on in that family."

Yvonne clasped Pauline's hand. "I'm still sad."

"You and me both," her aunt said.

Yvonne noticed the ring still on Pauline's finger. She raised the hand, nodding toward it. "Still wearing it?"

Auntie P. touched the lovely jewel. "I'm trying to talk my 'no' into being a 'not yet.'" She gave Yvonne a sad smile. "It may sound funny, but I think maybe Hank and I have some growing up to do."

Yvonne leaned her head against Pauline's shoulder. "Mama told me once you should never marry a man until you've had at least one good fight with him." It had turned out to be true where Neal was concerned. That horrible night of arguing over the dog in the road, a side of him had emerged that she'd never seen before. It was months of pain and disappointment until she could look at that discovery as a blessing. She would wish such pain and discovery away for Hank and Pauline, but it didn't work that way. *Can you make a way for her to be happy, Lord?* she prayed. *Show them the future You have for them?*

Contrary to Neal, the arguments she'd had with Chaz—if you could call their spats arguments—had made her admire Chaz more, not less. His true self that showed up in frustration or disappointment was a man of loyalty who felt his obligations deeply. She surprised herself by adding another prayer. *While You're at it, show Chaz the future You have for him.*

"Where is he? With Chaz?" Pauline asked as she walked away from the dessert table. She didn't need to clarify whom. Most of the guests noticed the empty place at Pauline's table. No one asked Auntie P. outright—town and family gossip had traveled fast enough to render the topic off-limits—but Hank's absence seemed to hang heavy in the air.

"I doubt he's with Chaz. Those two didn't strike me as ready to talk to each other this morning." Chaz had disappeared soon after the cake was transported and set in place at the venue. She could practically hear the gears turning in his head as he wrestled with the idea of Hank's offer of a visit. She wondered if he was out at the riverbank with Cecil again, hurling new rocks into the river.

Pauline's spine straightened a bit as the bride and groom kissed each other on the dance floor. "Will you go?"

She'd told Pauline about Hank's invitation. While she'd expressed surprise, Pauline had offered no advice for or against the visit.

Yvonne gave her aunt the same answer she'd given Chaz the several times he'd asked. "I don't know."

"I think you should."

Yvonne turned to look at Auntie P., not expecting that answer. "You do? You know he just wants to convince me to convince you."

"I know," Pauline replied. After a moment's pause, she added, "I guess there's a part of me that hopes he will."

That seemed like a heavy weight to place on the invitation to visit Wander Canyon. "How on earth will I know what to tell you?"

Pauline's arm slipped around Yvonne's shoulders. "Maybe you won't." She squeezed. "But you've got my open eyes and your own cautious heart. You think like me—" she leaned in "—but you won't be pulled under by those dreamy blue eyes." She gave a soft giggle like a teenager. "I just can't think clearly around that man, but maybe you can."

Advise anyone—especially Pauline—on matters of the Walker men? She was already finding it difficult to think clearly around a certain other man from Wander Canyon. The curmudgeon in Chaz Walker seemed to be disappearing in front of her own eyes. It had been much easier to spar with him over frosting choices than figure out what to do with the frost falling off the man's personality. The more time she spent with him, the more she liked him. The layers of his character fascinated her. His steadiness somehow steadied her. It made her wonder how pulled under she'd be if she ever saw the man genuinely happy. Or glimpsed him as smitten as Hank still appeared.

"You really think I should go?" It had seemed so outrageous at first, but the idea was actually starting to grow on her. And not just for Hank and Pauline's sake. A growing part of her wanted to see Chaz in the home he loved so much.

"You've got no van and no events coming up, and he's offering to pay your way. If that's not God paving a path, I don't know what is. If nothing else, you can make sure Chaz takes good care of Cecil."

Yvonne had no doubts Chaz would take excellent care of his new dog. But if Yvonne wasn't ready to admit anything about Chaz, Cecil was as good an excuse as any.

"Go," Pauline said, her eyes moist with the threat of tears. "Go for Cecil. Go for me. I'm worried about Hank. I know it sounds crazy, but I'll feel better if you're there."

Yvonne would do anything for Auntie P. Evidently *anything* was about to mean visiting Wander Canyon.

But not before a certain dog rolled down Aisle Avenue in tomorrow's pet parade.

*Oh, fella. I'm sorry.*

Chaz looked at poor Cecil as he turned the corner and silently promised the dog a steak. Or three.

Why had he ever agreed to Lulu and Carly's demand that he not see Cecil until he appeared in the parade?

Then again, why had he submitted to any of the strange requests and demands made of him since setting foot in the town of Matrimony Valley?

A low, giggling "oh, my" from Yvonne standing next to him only made it worse.

Cecil's scruffy head poked out of a giant collar of ruffly white fabric trimmed with red pom-poms. A lot of red pom-poms.

"What did they do to his nose?" He didn't bother to hide his mortification at the dog's brightly red-hued nose.

"I don't know," Yvonne said, still chuckling. "Lipstick, maybe?"

He let out a groan. "My dog is wearing lipstick."

"Well, we don't know for sure, and it's only his nose." Yvonne offered what he suspected she thought was an encouraging look. "It's cute."

*Cute.* Other people could have cute dogs,

but he was not one of them. One of the things that had first attracted him to Cecil was the sense of strength he got from the dog. A quiet grit, a determination to survive. Uncute qualities in his view, if such a thing existed.

Which this morning, it clearly did not. Enormous blue bows flopped from each of Cecil's ears, matching the—was that a child's cardigan sweater?—worn backward on his chest so that a stream of yellow buttons ran down the dog's back. A giant red pom-pom had been tied to his tail, so that the thing bounced back and forth as he wagged it.

And he *was* wagging it, which meant Cecil wasn't in anguish over this loss of doggy dignity, even though it made Chaz wince. In fact, if the amount of tail wagging could be believed, he'd have to say Cecil was enjoying this spectacle.

Thank goodness Dad didn't really know how to work the camera on his phone. If anyone so much as pondered the idea of sending photos of this back to Wander Canyon, he'd never live it down.

"Oh, look at how excited Carly and Lulu are," Yvonne pointed out as she touched his elbow. He tried not to notice the little zing that went through him whenever she touched him. He had to admire how hard she was working to pile up the positives for this crazy scheme.

The girls were dressed in matching outfits that looked just like Cecil's, right down to the big blue bows and painted red noses. They smiled enormous grins and waved enthusiastically as they pulled the dog along in the red wagon. Covered in blue and yellow streamers, the wagon now boasted giant cardboard wagon wheels taped over its regular wheels. The contraption did, in fact, bear a pretty impressive resemblance to a circus wagon.

"Kelly said she helped with the wagon, but the girls did the costumes all on their own." Yvonne's face wore the ear-to-ear smile he could never seem to get out of his mind. "I think they've got a real shot at the grand prize. Only Maureen Rogers's inchworm is better, if you ask me."

Earlier in the parade, someone had ingeniously attached a child's toy in halves to a dachshund. They'd somehow rigged the contraption so that the poor dog appeared to inch along the street as it walked. Personally, Chaz didn't see how anyone should be rewarded with a grand prize for doing this to defenseless animals. He seemed to be the only one with that opinion, however, because everyone else seemed to be having a great time.

To Chaz's horror, Yvonne raised her phone to snap a shot of Cecil. He fixed her with his best angry bull grunt and shook his head in a wordless *don't you dare* look. She glared right back—not many women on God's earth gave as good as they got like that—but lowered her phone and slipped it into her pocket.

And how many women made cinnamon buns so amazing and coffee so good he didn't mind the sugar she'd added? He should tell her he took it black, but it amused him to hold back the small secret. He'd miss this particular baker's talents. With a pinching sensation, he realized he'd now compare the cookies from his favorite spot back in Wander with Yvonne's. Maybe all cookies with Yvonne's. Maybe other things, too.

Once Cecil and most of the parade had passed by, Yvonne motioned for them to start walking toward Matrimony Falls and the gazebo where the parade would finish up and prizes would be announced.

"You made two little girls very happy today," she said as they walked.

"I suppose" was all he could manage through the tangle of his feelings.

Despite all the stress of the past few days, Yvonne somehow glowed in the strong sunlight. It did things to her hair. It bounced off her skin from the inside somehow. He knew her life was far from perfect at the moment, but she managed to still look so... happy. As if she generated her own internal sunshine. He was running out of ways to resist being drawn by that internal sunshine, mostly because he felt as if a storm cloud followed him everywhere.

"Have you decided?" he tried to ask casually while they were still a bit away from the crowd gathering in front of the gazebo. It startled him how much he wanted to know.

He hadn't expected Dad to show for the parade, but he'd been a bit surprised that Pauline had not joined them this morning. This seemed to be just her kind of quirky celebration. It told Chaz a lot that she wasn't here.

Yvonne said Pauline was tired from all the festivities and stress of yesterday's wedding, but he suspected it was just hard for her to be cheerful. After all, they were pres-

ently walking to the spot Pauline had told him many Matrimony Valley brides chose to get married.

She'd been planning her own wedding here when she told him that. That seemed enough to keep her away from this pretty little spot. Chaz had to admit, he'd grown fond of Pauline. She had strength, grit and determination, too. He really was coming to believe she'd have been good for Dad. His mother had always quoted the Bible verse about how "all things work together for good." God would have to work pretty hard to pull much good out of what was happening to these two families right now.

"I think I'm going to go." There was just the hint of a question in her tone, as if she was testing to see what he thought of the idea.

"Really?" He couldn't voice any of the thoughts and questions piled up behind that single word. Thoughts and questions that had kept him up half of last night. On one

hand, Yvonne's visit to Wander Canyon would feel like a pleasant but alarming invasion. It bugged him how quickly she had pushed her way into his life—and too many of his thoughts—without his permission.

"I asked Cathy if she wanted to try running the shop for a couple of days, and she was thrilled at the idea." Yvonne shrugged. "There are no events on my calendar, so I could go. I know I could use the break."

The ranch he called home was beautiful—breathtakingly so, in his opinion. But would Yvonne find it so? He'd be sure to have a mountain of catch-up troubleshooting to do, which might leave her listening to persuasive speeches from Dad. Or worse, Wyatt would abandon all tasks to go all ladies' man over Yvonne. Now, there was a prospect that truly annoyed him. He had no plans to add hogging Yvonne's time to his list of grievances against Wyatt.

"Fine dog you got there." Chaz recognized Kelly's husband, Bruce, from his res-

cue of them the night of the accident. He nodded in appreciation of the commiserating grin Bruce gave him. Now the father of two young girls, Bruce had likely endured his own share of girlie humiliation, Chaz suspected. "Tolerant animal."

Cecil had been astonishingly tolerant of whatever the girls wanted to do with him. Happy to have someone take good care of him, Chaz supposed. He'd become ridiculously fond of Cecil in the short time they'd been together. The idea of making all the arrangements for Cecil to fly home with him tomorrow no longer seemed impulsive or extreme; it felt absolutely necessary.

It reminded him of the time Dad had taken him to the horse market when he was twelve and bought his first mount. "How will I know which one to pick?" he'd asked his stepfather.

He'd never forgotten Dad's answer: "You don't choose the horse, son. The horse chooses you."

The echoing memory of Dad's voice saying "son" rang both jarring and familiar in his head.

Did Yvonne realize she'd tucked her hand into his elbow as she said "Here we go. I hope they win"?

Marvin from the ice cream shop cleared his throat as he stood next to a small table set with three trophies. "Welcome to Matrimony Valley's sixth annual pet parade." The crowd applauded as the entrants lined up next to the gazebo. "What a fabulous set of paraders we had this year."

Lulu and Carly beamed, waving right at him so enthusiastically that he felt he had to offer a small wave back. When Yvonne pulled her hand from his arm to wave back, he felt the loss of contact. *Get ahold of yourself, man. She's not for you, and you're definitely not for her.* They both laughed as Carly promptly planted a red-nosed kiss on Cecil's head, knocking off one of the colossal blue bows.

"Third place goes to Hilda Miller's parakeet, Molly." A woman who'd perched her yellow parakeet inside a hanging lantern on a staff and dressed like some character from a Dickens novel squealed and walked forward to accept her trophy.

"Second place goes to our newest canine visitor, Cecil."

Yvonne shouted and clapped as Lulu and Carly wheeled the wagon forward and accepted their trophy. They didn't seem at all upset not to have taken first place. He'd never mastered the ability to be satisfied with second place. Right now, the whole ranch succession thing was feeling like a giant second-place win at the moment, come to think of it.

True to Yvonne's prediction, Cecil was "inched out" of first place by the dachshund/inchworm. But as the awards ceremony broke up, knots of people gathered around all three pets, heaping congratulations on them equally. No one seemed to even care who won, just that everyone got to enjoy themselves.

Carly, the younger of the two girls, rushed up to Chaz, wrapping her arms around him even though she could barely reach above his belt buckle. "Thanks for letting us borrow Cecil!" she said, smiling up at him. His heart melted a bit. Maybe cute had its virtues.

It melted further still when Lulu clutched him from the other side so that he was sandwiched between little girls in clown costumes. "He's the best dog ever!" Lulu exclaimed, her smile as sweet as her sister's. Her *stepsister's*, he'd learned, for Bruce and Kelly were a blended family. "You're the best-est for bringing him here!"

The combination of being branded the best-est of anything, as well as the bittersweet kinship of two stepsisters, sank straight into his heart with a startling power. Chaz found himself momentarily speechless, caught off guard by how the pint-size hugs and praise affected him. His own family couldn't seem to fuse without friction, whereas this family seemed to be even better for the blending.

Catching Yvonne's expression as she watched him accept the hugs only made it worse. Or better.

Everyone in Matrimony Valley was so bafflingly odd. But they were also so disarmingly nice. He couldn't work out how those two things went together.

The only thing he could work out was the unsettling realization that he just might miss the place when he left. And how surprisingly grateful he was that one resident of the valley would be accompanying him home, even if for only a few days.

# Chapter Thirteen

*I'm here. I'm not sure why yet, Lord, but it
sure is beautiful!*

The flight information told Yvonne it
was fifteen hundred miles between Matrimony Valley and Wander Canyon, but as
she stepped out of the truck Monday afternoon, Yvonne felt as if she'd traveled to a
whole other world.

There was so much space. The Blue Ridge
Mountains of her home state were impressive, but Colorado's Rocky Mountains
somehow opened up into unfathomable
space here. She looked up at the impossi-
bly clear sky…and almost toppled over.

"Whoa there," Chaz said, grabbing her shoulder as the world spun a bit. "You're eight thousand feet up. Bit of a shock to your system at first." He handed her a second water bottle after insisting she down a first when they got off the plane. "You need to drink a lot at first."

She tried not to think about what it felt like to collapse—even for a second or two—against his chest. Every time they touched—even if only for a moment—his solid steadiness called to her. There was something rare about it, a treasure buried under all the gruff exterior he showed the rest of the world. She'd come to find it comforting amid the continually shifting storm of Hank and Pauline. "Do you ever feel it? When you go away and come back?"

Chaz pulled in a deep breath of the crisp mountain air she seemed to feel tingle all around her. "Not really. I'm used to it. Just feels like…home, I suppose."

She had to ask. "And what did the valley feel like?"

The twinkle in his eye delighted her. "I'd better not say."

He did look at home here. The tension that drew his shoulders tight all the time in Matrimony Valley had already eased up a bit. His familiarity with the ranch was obvious, but so was the hint that he was looking at it with new eyes. Embittered eyes, perhaps.

What did it feel like to cast his gaze across the land and know it would never be his? If she really did decide to leave Matrimony Valley, selling the family house would be the hardest part. But to have someone yank it out from under her the way Hank had done to Chaz? Yvonne couldn't fathom that kind of betrayal. The frosty distance between the two men had made the plane ride challenging. She wondered if half of Hank's reason for inviting her was just to keep the peace.

Chaz walked to the truck's bed and let

down the tailgate. "Welcome home, Cecil. You'll be running all over this place in no time." Unlocking the door to Cecil's crate, he easily scooped the large dog up in his arms and deposited him on the ground. "What do you think?"

Poor Cecil. He'd weathered the plane ride remarkably well. He hobbled around in energetic circles, barking and sniffing as if he wanted to race off in every direction. Then even he wobbled, making Yvonne crouch down to put her arms around the dog. "Still a little woozy from the flight, are you? You and me both."

"He should have a good long drink, too," Hank said. "Let's go into the main house."

Hank had explained that he and Wyatt resided in the ranch's main house. "Where Pauline oughta be living," he'd said wistfully. He'd been dropping little nuggets of Pauline's place in his life into almost every conversation. Yvonne wasn't sure of much about Hank, but she could be sure he very much loved Pauline. Then again, she'd been madly in love with Neal. How you felt about a person didn't necessarily change aspects of their character. *Show me what I need to see out here*, she prayed as she followed Hank into the big timber-framed home that sat at the end of the drive.

*Space*. That was the word that kept coming to her as Hank pushed open the wooden front door with rugged cast-iron hinges. *Everything has so much space to it here.* She loved the valley's close and comfortable feeling, but something about the sheer expanse of everything—even though they were in a canyon with mountains on both sides—spoke to her.

Cecil bounded into the house—well, as much as Cecil bounded into anything with a cast still on his leg. She'd become so fond of him, impressed at how he adapted—as if dogs limped all the time. He made circles around the furniture in the house's great room as Hank led them toward a bank of enormous southern-facing windows. The sunshine was radiant, burning brightly through the fall colors of the leaves on the mountainsides in view.

"Never felt a need to hang artwork," Hank said, noting what must have been her awed expression. "What could ever hope to match this?"

She had to agree. From this vantage point, she could see Wander Canyon Ranch spread out before her, running all the way to the foothills in wide-open splendor. For a surprising moment, she understood Hank's resistance to splitting up the acreage.

"Chaz," Hank said as he picked up her suitcase, "take Yvonne out on the deck while I put her things in Pauline's room."

Chaz raised an eyebrow at her as they both caught yet another declaration of Pauline's missing presence. As Hank went on up the stairs, Chaz pushed open the set of wood-framed glass doors that led out onto a large deck.

"He doesn't ask often, does he?"

"What?"

"Hank. He mostly tells. Rather than asks, I mean. Has he always been like that?"

Chaz pulled in a deep, weary breath. "Yep."

Yvonne walked to the railing, still reaching to take in the sheer magnitude of the place. "He asked me, you know. I still don't know quite what to make of that."

She regretted the words as Chaz's eyes darkened. He didn't say "He never asked me," but his expression silently shouted the bitter declaration.

"Good for you," he said in something close to a mumble.

"It's so beautiful here." It was. Breathtaking.

He walked up beside her and planted his hands on the railing. Their hands were mere inches apart. "It is."

The reverent tone in his words let her feel his love of the land. It must cut so deep to be denied ownership on account of something so arbitrary as bloodline. From everything she'd heard, Chaz was more Walker than Wyatt was.

Then again, she hadn't even met Wyatt yet, so was it fair to judge? Family dynamics could make such a mess of everything— on mountains or in valleys.

She turned to consider Chaz. He appeared a completely different man here. He was already more calm and settled than the irritated fish out of water she'd gotten to know in Matrimony Valley. The man she was starting to know back there would come into full view out here. If a man could suit a place, Chaz Walker suited Wander Canyon. Was the opposite true of Wyatt? It seemed impossible to think she could ever hope to understand Hank's viewpoint.

Despite the rush to visit, one thing had continually rung true: coming here hadn't been an impulsive mistake. Wander Canyon had things to tell her—things both she and Pauline needed to know.

"I think I get it now," she admitted.

Chaz furrowed his eyebrows. "Get what?"

"Why the valley looks so small and…" She searched for the right word for how he viewed the valley's nonstop interaction. "…busy to you."

He stared at her for a moment, catching up to her thinking. "I do like my space," he said with a small laugh as he turned back to the landscape. It was always fun to watch people be awed by the beauty of Matrimony Falls, but Yvonne felt as if she could literally watch Chaz drink in this view. He gulped it down in big, healing doses.

Cecil had maneuvered the wide steps off the deck to do a three-legged dash around the yard, taking in all the new scents and smells. "Cecil seems to like all the space, too."

He gave a low chuckle. The laugh she thought would never come those first days in the valley seemed to come more easily lately. "That dog's gonna run like the wind once he gets that cast off."

"I'm amazed how fast he is already." She peered off to either side as Cecil traveled the length of the small fenced-in house yard, spying what must be the Wander Canyon Ranch herd. Only…

"Wait…" She leaned over the railing, squinting. She blinked, then blinked again. She couldn't be seeing that right. Those seemed to be cows. They were the right size to be cows, and some even had horns, but they looked more like giant, meandering sheepdogs. "Your cows…" she began, not quite sure how to say it. "They're…"

"Our *cattle*, you mean," he teased, one corner of his mouth curved up in a smile.

Yvonne turned back toward him. "Your cattle are shaggy!"

He looked as if he'd been waiting for her to notice, anticipating her astonishment. "We breed Scottish Highland cattle. And yes, while the correct term is 'long-haired,' I think 'shaggy' just about covers it."

He enjoyed their banter as much as she did. It changed his whole face, brought a new handsomeness to his features that she wasn't quite sure how to handle.

"They're adorable."

That brought a full laugh from Chaz. "I don't know that I'd go so far as to say they're adorable, but they're sturdy, low-maintenance and even-tempered."

"Things I can only imagine you prize in livestock." *And people, I'd venture.* If Hank was as much like Chaz as she suspected he was, there must be real truth to the idea that opposites attract. Some might call Auntie P. sturdy, but no one would use the words *low-maintenance* or *even-tempered.*

"I'm happy with our herd, yes. We've had a good year."

She stared out again at the unusual animals, completely fascinated. "What's the advantage of all that hair? I mean, there must be one." Chaz didn't seem like the kind to put up with a showy breed unless there was an advantage.

"A lot of their value is in their temperament and resilience. But the hair? It means they need less fat to keep them warm, so the meat is leaner, which people seem to like these days." The glint returned to his eyes as he added, "And people find them adorable."

She laughed, and the air between them seemed to warm. She was, in fact, very glad to be here. And maybe Hank had been wise to bring her here—these would be a cantankerous couple of days between Chaz, Wyatt and Hank. If they had to keep things civil in front of company, maybe it would help.

"Can I see one? Up close?"

"I'll take you out tomorrow. But I warn you, they're not as adorable up close. Some of them are downright...curmudgeonly." The word had become a joke between them.

She crossed her arms over her chest and leaned against the railing. "Imagine that."

She wanted to keep him talking, to encourage this unfolding of the closed-up person he'd been in the valley. "Have you always raised Scottish Highland cattle?"

Yvonne winced inwardly as the question wiped the smile from his face. "Actually, it was Wyatt's idea to add the Scots about five years ago. I'll admit, I dismissed it as classic Wyatt showmanship. Just another way to stand out and to grab attention."

"But?"

"Scots actually have a lot of good qualities."

"So Wyatt was right about them?"

If begrudging had a sound, it was the grunt Chaz emitted at that statement.

"Let's just say I can count the times I've agreed with one of Wyatt's wild schemes on one hand, and the Scots turned out to be one of them."

There was a heap of history behind those words. "So it's been successful?"

He let out another of those grunts. "*We've* managed the herd well enough to become one of the top breeders in the state."

He spit the *we've* out with such effort that Yvonne could see he felt the herd's reputation had been mostly his doing. The two brothers really were at tremendous odds with each other. Try as she might, she couldn't see how Hank thought giving one the ranch over the other would fix that. She couldn't see how it would do anything but just make it all worse.

Barking, Cecil took another lumbering lap around the fenced-in yard. She followed his path, looking to take in more of the ranch. It seemed to go on forever in every direction. There were half a dozen outbuildings, but nothing that looked like a second residence. "Where's your house?"

He pointed off to the left. "Back around that corner." Chaz held her gaze for a long moment before adding, "My house is behind this one."

His eyes told her he was talking about a lot more than just the sight lines.

He was glad she was here.

He was bothered she was here.

Chaz tried to sort through the continual flip-flop of his feelings as he unpacked and chose the perfect corner of his bedroom for Cecil's new bed.

He'd had to buy a duffel bag from the outfitters in Matrimony Valley for all of Cecil's stuff, not to mention an airline travel crate from Doc Mullins's veterinary office. There was something to how easily and impulsively he bought things for the dog, but he was in no hurry to figure out what it was. Surely Yvonne would be spouting opinions at some point.

"What do you think, boy?"

Cecil licked his hand, fetching the tug-of-war toy that had quickly become the dog's favorite.

"Not now. Dinner'll be soon and I've got to see how things have gotten on while we've been gone." He grabbed the hand-tooled leather folder he always carried his daily ranch papers in and headed down toward the small office on the first floor of his house.

The sight of Wyatt's truck in the driveway stopped him at the window on the landing.

*Wyatt.* He should have been here when they arrived, should have been ready to bring Chaz up to speed as to how the ranch had operated while he was gone. But, of course, he wasn't. It was just like Wyatt to be gone for the necessary stuff but to show up for dinner.

He halted halfway down the stairs. *Does he know?* Had Dad told him of his succession plans? He'd hoped Dad did him the courtesy of telling him first and Wyatt second, but Chaz felt like he could no longer predict Dad's behavior. Everything was up for grabs, and none of it to his liking.

What would Yvonne think of Wyatt? What would Wyatt think of Yvonne, for that matter? His brother would likely turn the charm on full blast for a pretty woman like Yvonne. He filed away how much that bugged him under "things I don't want to think about right now" and continued down the stairs.

Cecil followed right on his heels—his worry about how the dog would handle the open stairway of his timber-framed home proved unnecessary—and went straight to the front door, barking at the knock they both heard.

Wyatt was no doubt here to gloat about his newfound ranch-owner status. Pile that on top of the list of things that had gone undone while he was in North Carolina, and Chaz was primed for a fight. *Bring it on.* It was probably better to have it out over here away from Hank and Yvonne anyway.

Chaz made no point of hiding his scowl as he yanked the door open…to Yvonne's raised hand.

Cecil ducked around him to greet Yvonne with happy licks. Chaz was glad the welcome gave him a few seconds to swallow back down his ready rage.

It simply wasn't fair what the sunshine did to her hair and skin. It was as if she changed the air around her wherever she went, and he was starting to like getting caught up in that wake. Maybe even crave it a bit. Given the thousand-plus miles and familial knots between them, that was dangerous, wasn't it?

She smiled and shrugged. "I wanted to see your house. Plus, Wyatt and your dad are talking."

*I can just imagine.* "It's just like the big house. Only smaller." Her. In his space. Was he ready for that?

She caught his resistance. "Well, sure, but…"

It would take only a minute or two and maybe it was a better idea than sending her back there with Dad and Wyatt. And despite liking solitude and the privacy of his own space, his mama didn't raise him to be a complete...*curmudgeon.* "C'mon in."

She walked in toward the open living room, eyes wide as they had been in the other house. "It is. Only it's different." She touched his favorite leather chair, and he felt it as if she'd run her fingers over his arm. "Simpler. More like you. But still—" she pulled in a deep breath "—so much space."

"I like my space." He'd said that before— as an explanation of sorts. It felt like more of an admission now. As if it told her something private about him, which made no sense at all.

"Apart from them."

She got it. He wasn't sure how he knew that from the way she said those three words, but she got it. It felt like it had been far too long since anyone understood him. He used to think Dad did.

"So you like it? You're happy here?"

He walked into the room and stood by the mantel of the stone fireplace. "Most days I'm glad for it. Dad knew I needed my own space away from the big house."

She raised one eyebrow as she picked up a terra-cotta bowl that had been Mom's from its place on the coffee table. "And on the other days?"

"I'm in the guesthouse on my own land. Take a guess." Only soon enough it wouldn't be his own land, would it? How did she do that to him? One minute he was grasping for words; the next private things were tumbling out of him.

He watched her tuck that admission away without replying. Instead, she returned the bowl to the table and walked to the window that framed a view of the big house. "I met Wyatt."

Her tone was uncharacteristically unreadable, forcing him to ask, "And?"

"He talks a lot more than you do."

Of course he did. Wyatt was all words and little action. Useful when hiring or selling or getting something from the town council, but not much else.

Yvonne gave him a direct look. "He knows. He knew before you did."

She seemed to find that as unfair as he did. She understood. It struck him in a very scary way how hungry he'd become to be understood. His jaw ached, and he realized he'd been clenching his teeth.

She turned her gaze back to the big house. "I'll be honest, Chaz. I'm looking for the man Auntie P. fell for, and I'm not seeing him." She paused for a moment before adding, "I'm still not sure why I'm here."

*You and me both.* "Dad's pulling out all the stops to change Pauline's mind. He thinks you can do that."

She laughed. "I can no more do that than

you can change Hank's mind." She walked toward the counter that separated the great room space from his kitchen. Other people would wait to be led through a house, but evidently Yvonne was just fine exploring on her own. Did bakers pass judgment on other people's kitchens the way he evaluated other people's cattle? He followed her, nerves rising for no good reason.

Her eyes swept around the space. "Very tidy."

*Tidy* was a fussy, female word. He was organized. He disliked clutter. The exact opposite of Wyatt, not that he'd point that out at the moment.

"Do you cook?"

That sounded like a loaded question, like there was a right and wrong answer in her view. He settled for "Some," then qualified it by saying, "Dad has a cook at the big house, so most times it's easier for me to go over and get dinner there."

She made that little *hmm* noise. The one

she did while thinking. He wasn't sure he wanted to know what she thought of his cooking or kitchen, but he held back an audible wince when she opened his refrigerator and peered inside. This woman had nerve to spare; that was certain. He might be eager to be understood, but not to be invaded.

"You can tell a lot about someone by what's in their fridge." She said it as if the theory excused her nosiness.

Try as he might, he couldn't stop himself from asking, "And what does mine tell you?"

She began running her hands over the shelves the way she'd run her hands over his leather chair, and it practically made his skin itch. "Three kinds of hot sauce—well, that says something right there, doesn't it?"

"Like what?" When had he become so curious to know what she thought?

"Very particular, strong, determined."

The fact that it was true didn't give him any satisfaction whatsoever.

"Not what I'd expect from a man who told me vanilla is his favorite flavor." She looked up from her inspection of his fridge. "You surprise me, Chaz Walker."

He was inexplicably glad of that. It felt like she knew too much about him already.

# Chapter Fourteen

Yvonne yawned and batted her eyes open to the surprise of full sunlight. A quick glance at the clock showed it to be 7:30 a.m.—later than she had woken in months. The clear air seemed to make sleep easy, and the complexities of dinner the night before had been exhausting.

She pulled on her bathrobe and padded to the large window, looking out over the same impressive expanse of land she had seen from the deck.

Walker land. Wander Canyon Ranch. She was staring at a battleground for the two

Walker sons—and maybe their father or even her aunt.

It was hard to imagine Wyatt and Chaz in the same family. The two Walker sons were astonishingly different. Wyatt was blond, agile and talkative, with his father's light blue eyes and broad shoulders. Both men were handsome, but Chaz's looks were quiet and dark while Wyatt's were loud and gleaming.

Dinner had been delicious, but taxing. The continual undercurrent of sparring between Chaz and Wyatt made it hard to enjoy the food. There were moments where she felt more like a referee than a houseguest, scrambling just as hard as Hank to keep conversation light and out of the battle zone.

What conversations had happened after she'd pleaded a long day of travel and went upstairs to bed? Had the brothers argued? Given in to the accusations she'd sensed boiling just under the conversation all night long?

If they hadn't, they would. And soon. She wasn't sure she wanted to be anywhere near them when they did.

When Chaz had told her to be ready at nine to go out and see the herd, Wyatt balked. "I should take her out," he asserted, without offering any reason why.

"Yvonne will ride out with me," Chaz countered. "I'm sure you've got work to do." It had the tone of an accusation.

"And you don't? You've been gone with Dad for days."

Honestly, they were like preschoolers fighting over a new toy. She did prefer to spend the time with Chaz, but at that moment Yvonne considered asking Hank to show her the herd and break up the fight. *Oh, Auntie P., it's best you steer clear of all of this.*

"Let Chaz take Yvonne out to see the herd,

Wyatt," Hank had declared. "You and I have things to go over tomorrow morning."

Nine o'clock would come fast enough, so she showered and dressed in a top and jeans. She yanked on the boots Hank had told her to bring and pulled her hair back into a ponytail. "This is as ranch ready as I get," she told her reflection in the mirror. On a whim, she took a shot of herself in front of the window and its spectacular view and sent it to Pauline.

Pauline replied within a minute: How many arguments so far?

None outright, loads boiling under the surface, she replied back. Chaz taking me out to see the land today.

Take photos. Take care. Love you, came Auntie P.'s reply.

Just as she finished a luxuriously large cup of coffee and a bowl of yogurt with granola, Chaz walked into the kitchen, Cecil loping along behind him. He looked more rugged than he had in the valley—a little dusty, less on edge. A man clearly in his element, which was a very good look for him.

He poured himself a cup of coffee, and she shot him a dubious look when he passed up the sugar bowl. "I thought you didn't take it black."

The banter she was coming to enjoy bubbled up between them. "I *usually* take it black."

She smirked, entertained by his eyes. "Just not in Matrimony Valley?"

He leaned back against the counter. "Just not in arguments about cakes."

"That argument wasn't about cake."

He took a long drink of his coffee without taking his gaze from her. She felt the look hum under her skin. "True. Ready to see what all the fuss is about?"

He said it with a playful air, but she could see through it easily to a truer version of the question—one that was closer to "Ready to see why this hurts so much?" Through all the posturing and one-upmanship of last night's dinner, one thing had come through loud and clear: each of the three Walker men loved this land, just in very different ways.

She loved the valley, but it was the people she loved, not necessarily the land. Her sense of home wasn't tied to geography. Was that why she could envision leaving Matrimony Valley—in fact, she already was thinking about leaving?

Leaving Wander Canyon seemed like an impossible concept to Hank or Chaz. It was clear to her that no matter what stipulations Hank put on Chaz, no matter how dissatisfied Chaz was with whatever role Hank gave him, or even how fiercely the men argued, Chaz wouldn't leave Wander. This morning, knowing what she knew, she couldn't say if that was a good thing.

Chaz drained his cup and gave a small whistle, snapping Cecil's head immediately to attention. "Okay, then, we're off."

She grabbed her jacket off the kitchen

chair as he motioned toward the side door from which he'd entered.

She wasn't expecting the all-terrain vehicle parked on the grass.

He caught her surprise. "What?"

"I guess I was expecting the full-blown ranch-on-horseback thing." She felt foolish, as if she'd tripped over some cowboy stereotype. "You did say 'ride out with me.'" The moment the words left her lips, she realized it could easily mean the vehicle in front of her. And she could hardly expect Cecil to keep up if they were on horseback.

"Do you ride?" He looked at her as if he already knew the answer to that question.

"I look fabulous atop a carousel pony," she countered in a failed attempt to keep some sort of upper hand.

He simply laughed at that. "We've got one in town, believe it or not—with way more than ponies on it, actually. But I was talking about the live kind."

"Well, then, no. Not really."

Chaz eased himself into the driver's seat. "Well, then, this is better. For your safety, Cecil's leg and your ability to sit down comfortably for the next two days. We're going a bit of a distance."

She climbed into the passenger side. "You make a good point."

He started the engine, and Cecil hopped into the back seat as if he'd lived on Wander his whole life. The dog stuck his tongue out and panted with such goofy enthusiasm that she couldn't help but laugh herself.

"I'll make you a deal," Chaz said as he turned the vehicle toward the grassy land beyond the house fence. "I'll take you for a test drive on both the live kind and our carousel in town later. But for now we'll use the four-wheel version."

Yvonne tried to imagine Chaz Walker on a carousel and nearly burst out in new laughter. After all, the man had barely been able to stomach a pet parade. "Deal."

* * *

Chaz pointed to where the edge of Wander Canyon Ranch met up with the national park at the foot of the mountains. "It goes all the way to there."

Yvonne tented her eyes with her hand, letting out an awestruck sound as her gaze followed his gesture. "All that way?"

She'd been making that sound all morning. He couldn't figure out why he liked hearing it so much until he realized he'd *wanted* her to be impressed. He wanted her to understand the value of this land—and its meaning to him. He wasn't just some ungrateful, spiteful stepson crying foul over a decision Dad had every legal right to make. Of course he could cite the same logical reasons as Dad as to why the land should stay intact. The biology that made Wyatt a full-blooded Walker, and him just an adopted son, would never change. An objective observer could see the reason in Dad's chosen course of action.

He wasn't an objective observer. As far as he was concerned, he'd been told to sacrifice his heart in the name of some faulty sense of family bloodline.

He couldn't swallow that as fair. Wouldn't ever swallow that as fair. And some insistent part of him needed her to see that.

After a moment or two, she finally turned back toward him, her eyes as serious as he'd ever seen them. "Isn't there room enough for both of you here?"

There wasn't a more dangerous question. True to this woman's direct nature, it cut to the very heart of everything. It was the one question he could barely stand to hear from her—or from anybody. It was the question he shouted at Dad that first night home and the one he'd thrown in Wyatt's face.

Was there room for both him and Wyatt? Did his happiness matter more than the benefits of keeping the land intact? Why didn't he matter as much as any other Walker? Those and a dozen other questions banged around the dark corners of his house last night. His *separate* house—which in itself hinted at the answer, didn't it?

"I don't know," he finally replied. "I used to think so. I used to believe that Wyatt and I could be equal partners, genuine brothers." He hadn't expected the words to cut so deep as he spoke them.

"What will you do?" How did she make her words sound so soft? How had she gotten so far under his skin so fast?

He picked up a rock. He needed to touch something—either the land or her—and the land was the far safer choice at that moment. His mind cast back to standing on the riverbank in North Carolina pitching lug nuts. That was the first moment he'd entertained the insane notion that he might have something to offer her. Foolishness. "You make it sound like I have a choice."

"Don't you? I mean, don't you always have a choice? You could walk away."

"No." He could do lots of things, but walk

away from Wander Canyon Ranch wasn't ever one of them. He'd stay and endure all of it. "No, I couldn't leave."

She was sitting on a fallen tree trunk, and she pulled her knees up to hug them, ready to listen. "Why?" He didn't want to talk about it, but she had this way of poking at his resistance until she cracked it open.

"Because he knows that. Dad knows I'll agree to whatever keeps me on the ranch. So he's fixed it so that Wyatt can't walk away because he knows I never will. What's the point of being loyal if all it gets you is second place?"

Her face changed, as if she'd just realized something huge. "Do you think Hank loves Wyatt more than you?"

What was it with this woman and her questions? "Of course he does!" The words came shouting from some unleashed part of himself, strong and shameful. How did Yvonne yank things out of him he didn't want revealed?

"Well, maybe not," he amended, only because it sounded so terrible to leave hanging in the open like that. He couldn't bear her to see the truth in his outburst.

Even though he knew his backpedal hadn't fooled her, she let the subject drop. He was grateful for the grace of her silence, for the time and space he needed to wrestle his temper back under control. He hadn't expected her to understand—or respect—his need for quiet like that. Yvonne kept surprising him. Usually, he didn't like that in a person.

Cecil's bark and a chorus of low moos announced the arrival of the herd behind them, and Yvonne turned in childlike delight.

"They really do say 'moo'!" She laughed.

"They're cows," he said. "Well, cows and bulls."

"But they all have horns. Big ones." She looked rather grateful for the fence between them.

"The females—cows—sweep out and up, while the males—bulls—go horizontal, then turn up at the tips." He pointed out the difference as one cow meandered up to the fence and gave a loud, declarative moo of hello.

"The hair," she exclaimed in that awestruck tone that was steadily working its way under his skin. "That nose. They're adorable."

He wasn't sure *adorable* was the right word for a thousand pounds of livestock, but he let her enjoy the encounter as the cow pushed her square black nose over the fence. "Too bad you're not here during calf season. That's when they are adorable. They look a bit like teddy bears."

Her smile absolutely glowed. "What's her name? It's a her, right?" The cow mooed again, longer this time, and Yvonne giggled as if she were Lulu and Carly back at the pet parade.

"We don't name them. They're not pets."

It was better not to name your dinner, Dad had told him the first time he'd attempted to name one of the calves.

"Look at all the different colors!" He liked the wonder in her eyes. It soothed him somehow.

The herd had mostly the reddish-brown variety, but a few of them were black, cream or brindle, and there were even a pair of white ones this year. Yvonne stepped closer, her hand outstretched toward the comical nose beneath all that shaggy hair.

He dashed toward her, cursing the fascination that had pulled his guard down around the animals. "Take care. She doesn't..."

Too late. The cow swung her enormous head, and Yvonne yelped while diving back out of the way of the horns. They weren't sharp, but they were large enough to do damage. She went tumbling backward, but not before he caught her.

She was tiny. Small and light and wispy, as if he could catch her with one hand. Only he had her in both arms. For a split second, he couldn't tell if her wide eyes were from surprise or from the feelings rushing through him at their contact. It took no effort at all to hold her. No, the effort required was to breathe, because he couldn't seem to pull in a proper breath with her staring at him like that.

It felt embarrassingly long before he finally gulped out, "You okay?"

"Yeah, sure." The breathless tone in her voice felt like the hollow in his chest. Like the tone of Hank's words when he talked about Pauline.

A curl of panic gripped him as he helped her upright, and something he couldn't name slipped out of his grasp, out of his control, as she escaped his arms. He wanted to pull her back, to freeze that moment, as potent as it was dangerous. "You need to be more careful around livestock," he said in the most practical tone he could muster with a small tornado going off in his chest.

"Good to remember." Her awestruck tone took on a whole new timbre, which only added to his panic. It was there, between them. They were doing their best to ignore it, or deny it, but he could already tell that was going to work for only so long.

"So, that's the herd and the ranch." The absurd pronouncement made him want to whack his head.

"I see why you love it so much." She seemed as desperate to fill the air between them with words as he was. He brushed something off the hood of the vehicle while she straightened her hair for no good reason. "It's beautiful."

He'd felt her hair brush against his forearm when he'd held her. That same forearm tingled now, as if every single detailed memory left a mark. Chaz whistled for Cecil, and the dog hopped in behind the front seats. "We should head back. Lunch will be ready, and then we'll head into town."

"Sure," she said a bit too brightly as she

settled herself into the passenger seat. "No problem at all."

There was where she was wrong. Because he didn't like the idea of her being anywhere in Wander—anywhere in Colorado, for that matter—without him, and that was a very big problem indeed.

# Chapter Fifteen

Something was seriously wrong with him.

Chaz stood outside the building that held the Wander Canyon Carousel a few hours later and wondered if he'd left his good sense in North Carolina. He had a million other things—important things—that he ought to be doing this afternoon, but all he wanted to do was show Yvonne around the town he called home.

It was bad enough that he'd spent the last half hour sampling cookies and coffee drinks from the coffee shop next to the carousel. Now he was about to willingly get on the ride. Without a small child involved. *I'm insane.*

It was that confounded look of wonder in her eyes that rendered him defenseless. He couldn't get enough of it, would do anything to see it light up her eyes the way it did right now. She gaped at the building, astonished. "I admit, I thought you were kidding about the carousel."

"Nope. This is our carousel." He pointed to the framed print on the wall that told the story of the ride's history. "A local guy who'd had a bad time of it in World War II decided to build it a ways back. Been here in town ever since."

At the moment, he realized the true consequence of this ridiculous impulse: it was public. He knew far too many people in Wander Canyon for something like this to go unnoticed. The look of shock on the ticket taker's face proved Chaz right.

He tried to buy two tickets with a casual air, as if thirty-year-old men rode carousels all the time. He even threw an extra five dollars into the tip jar that supported a different local charity each month. It didn't lessen the attendant's wide-eyed stare any less.

Did his presence here have to be such a shocking concept? Did it have to feel like the whole world could somehow see the light-headed feeling he got around Yvonne?

After all, Wyatt often brought dates here. Given the chance, Wyatt would probably try to bring her here, which was exactly why he wasn't going to give Wyatt that chance. *He* wanted to be the one to bring her here. For a shuddering moment, he realized he felt the way Dad looked around Pauline— and that was bad news indeed.

Chaz pushed open the small gate that led into the room housing the indoor carousel. Unable to stop himself, he turned so that he could fully catch Yvonne's reaction. The woman practically glowed with delight, as if she'd turned into a five-year-old in front of his eyes. "Oh my goodness!" One hand went to her chest as she walked around the ride. He hadn't thought her eyes could get wider.

Granted, this was no ordinary merry-go-round. The Wander Carousel hosted a crazy assortment of unusual mounts. Fish, sheep, an enormous bluebird, even an octopus— but no ponies. Every local kid got to ride the carousel free on their birthday. It had become the unofficial symbol of Wander Canyon.

"Which one do you ride?" she asked as if he rode frequently.

He scratched his chin. Truthfully, he couldn't remember the last time he'd been on the carousel, or even taken someone else to ride it. "It's been a few years."

The attendant gave a small cough and attempted to blend into the paneling. He'd tried to choose a time when there would be lots of other people here, but to no avail. They were getting the ride to themselves, it looked like. No one and nothing to diffuse her attention or his visibility. *I may never live this down.*

"Which one did you ride *when you rode*?" she persisted, narrowing her eyes at him. "I have a guess, and I want to see if I'm right."

He felt absurd admitting it, but said, "The octopus."

She pointed at him. "I knew it!" She ran a hand along one of the curly tentacles, and he felt it under his skin the same way he had when she touched his furniture. "He's gorgeous. Fabulous choice."

He crossed his hands over his chest, desperate to feel less like a smitten idiot. "And how do you know it's a he?"

Yvonne laughed. "Because *you'd* never ride a girl octopus." Then she pointed to something he'd never noticed before. "And he's wearing a little bow tie."

Chaz had ridden this carousel dozens of times when he was younger. How had he never noticed that his favorite ride wore a bow tie? She'd been in Wander Canyon not even two days and was showing him things about his home he didn't know. She even peeled back things about himself he didn't know. Would the dueling sensations of fear and fascination ever leave him in this woman's presence?

She stepped up onto the round platform. "Well, then, seems I have to ride the bluebird."

"No, you don't," he countered quickly. "You can ride whatever animal you want."

She climbed onto the bird. "Oh, no. I want a front-row view to Chaz Walker riding a carousel octopus."

The wobbly, tinny tones of the carousel's organ signaled the ride was about to start, and Chaz had no choice but to haul himself up onto the wooden beast and attempt not to look like an idiot.

She looked perfectly…*adorable* atop the chubby blue creature, her eyes as big and round as the bird's. Somehow he knew the vision of her gleefully perched atop a carousel bluebird would be stuck in his mind for years to come.

Yvonne cocked her head to one side. "Suits you."

He held back a smile. "I doubt that."

She only laughed, and continued laughing as the music swelled and the ride cranked into gear.

He tried not to laugh. He tried to stay upright and dignified and stare at anything but her exuberance. *Joy.* The man who'd seen such wartime horror said he'd built the carousel to bring joy into the world. The woman beside him was struggling to keep her bakery afloat, had just ruined her aunt's wedding, had her car totaled and was being pressured by Dad, and yet she was riding a giant bluebird as if they were flying through the clouds.

She had so much joy. Was that it? The reason he couldn't get her out of his thoughts? Was that what fed his growing continual craving to have her nearby? To know what she thought of just about everything?

They went around and around, her laughter eventually making him laugh. He felt himself surrender to the dizzy, off-kilter feeling in his gut that had nothing to do with the rotations of the carousel.

When the music stopped, she turned to him and said in complete seriousness, "Can we go around again?"

Who was the man inside his skin who said "Sure"?

She climbed down off the bluebird and began wandering through the rows to choose a new animal to ride. "Oh, this one!" she exclaimed at a dramatic rooster and climbed on.

Had she chosen it because she liked the brilliant colors, or the fact that it placed him on the giant porcupine next to it?

"Happy coincidence." She met his dubious expression with a mischievous grin. "Mount up." She settled in, clipping the small rope belt he'd always found a hopelessly optimistic "safety feature" around her waist. The riotous thought of what his hands would feel like around her waist poked into his brain, and he tried to shake it off.

"Or you can always choose something else. You don't have to ride next to me. I mean, every other animal is free." They were, in fact, still alone in the building. He could ride any one of the animals. She seemed to know he wouldn't.

No, he was determined to ride right next to Yvonne Niles. Wild horses—or any other beast on this carousel—wouldn't stop him from watching her ride. As the ride started up again, Chaz realized he'd empty his wallet for a dozen rides to keep seeing that look in her eyes.

It had been the most amazing day.

The scenery was breathtaking, the town of Wander Canyon was charming, and even the food had been delicious. Of course, her absolute favorite thing had been the carousel. One moment wouldn't stop replaying in her mind. Chaz had reached up to help her get down off an enormous comical grasshopper, lifting her effortlessly by the waist. He'd deposited her down close next to him, and they froze there, stunned by sheer proximity.

She told herself the dizzy sensation was due to the altitude. Or the rotations of the carousel. That it was anything but the helpless look in his eyes. Anything but the way her breath caught. She told herself the Walker men were an emotional minefield, that she was here for Pauline. That her heart had been pulled under before and couldn't be trusted, especially not now. She'd been grateful when he broke away, when he looked as flustered as she felt.

It was as if they didn't know how to talk to each other after that. They made bumbling small talk on the drive back to the ranch, arriving in time to wash up before dinner. Wyatt had stopped in for a quick update that seemed to irritate Chaz, then headed off somewhere in town, missing dinner. Chaz had eaten with her and Hank, but quickly pleaded a mountain of ranch tasks and headed off toward the barns after the meal.

Now she stood on the deck alone with Hank. The man handed her another glass of water as he settled himself into the chair opposite her. "Keep drinking up. It helps with the altitude. I know you live near the mountains, but—" he gestured to the stunning view "—we tend to grow them a bit higher over here."

The sunset painted them in colors far different from her mountains from home. "They are beautiful. It's all beautiful. And the cows."

The older man laughed. "The unusual breed was Wyatt's idea. Chaz took a heap of convincing. Said he wanted to raise cattle, not stuffed animals. Course, I hear you rode the carousel today, so you can see how maybe that fits right in."

"I suppose I can." She could easily see how Chaz fit into this canyon. It made it that much harder to understand why Hank had made the decision he had. Part of her wanted to shout, "How on earth could you think that would work?"

"Pauline would have me send her photos almost every day," Hank reminisced, gesturing out at the grand view. "The mountains or some patch of flowers or the cattle." He swallowed hard. "She'd love living here, and that's a fact."

She would—the ranch, at least. The squabbling family, maybe not so much. For a woman with no children of her own, who'd been the independent, adventurous family outlier, Pauline cared a great deal about family harmony. She'd always been the peacemaker in Yvonne's family, pressing Mama all the time for how much Yvonne and her sisters couldn't seem to get along. She and her aunt were so much alike that for the longest time Yvonne always thought Auntie P. was on her side. It was only as she grew older that Yvonne realized Auntie P. was on *everybody's* side.

Except, of course, Neal's. There, Pauline fully supported Yvonne's view that there was no reconciling. One strike, relationship over.

Hank leaned in toward Yvonne with intense eyes, bringing her thoughts back to the present. "I love her to the moon and back, you know."

It was easy to see that he did. But was it enough? In this family? Hank clearly wanted her to step in and be the peacemaker between himself and Pauline. How could she when she wasn't convinced herself?

"Do you blame me?" she blurted out, suddenly needing to know.

"I respect a woman who speaks her mind,"

he replied. "I know you think you're protecting your aunt."

Yvonne felt her gut tighten at the all-too-familiar words. Neal had professed the same respect for an opinionated woman—until that woman's opinion clashed with his. Did her current doubts mean she was learning to recognize red flags? Or was she letting her history with Neal influence what she thought of Hank?

And then there was this growing urge to defend Chaz. She couldn't seem to tamp down her outrage at the injustice of it all. He'd been so loyal. The land meant so much to him. She'd told herself she came out here to find out about Hank for Pauline. Today made her realize part of her had come to find out about Chaz for herself.

*So speak up.*

Yvonne turned her chair so that it faced Hank head-on. It was time to ask the real question. After all, she'd never actually asked Hank directly, only heard Chaz's version. "Why hand down the ranch this way? Why create all this pain and bad feelings between brothers?"

Hank seemed to have been waiting for her to ask. "Because keeping it in one piece with Wyatt is the right thing for Wander Canyon Ranch."

She couldn't believe that, and gave him a skeptical look.

His eyes cooled with a determination that looked so much like Chaz's. Wyatt may have favored Hank in appearance, but Chaz's personality mirrored Hank's in so many ways. "It was—is—the hardest decision I've ever had to make. But it's the right one, and I stand by it."

Yvonne pulled one of Pauline's favorite peacekeeping phrases from the vault of her memory. "Help me understand."

Hank made the same pained grunting sound she'd heard Chaz make and pulled himself from the chair. He walked to the railing and leaned back against it to face her. Standing against the backdrop of the land, he looked part of it, as though he'd grown there with deeply sunk roots like a tree. *Walker land.* "I suppose Chaz told you this whole mess is about the Walker bloodline. About how I must consider him some sort of second-class son. Have I got it about right?"

His frank words surprised her. She didn't know how much to admit. "Something like that."

Hank scratched his chin and tucked one hand in his pocket. "Well, that's not the reason."

A part of her was a little relieved to hear him say that. She didn't want to think the man who'd captured Auntie P.'s heart could be so cruel. "Why, then?"

"The short answer is that Wyatt needs the land and Chaz doesn't."

That seemed the exact opposite of what she'd seen today. She'd soaked in the way Chaz looked at the ranch, couldn't help but notice the longing in his eyes as they rode across the landscape this morning. *Need* seemed like exactly the right word for how Chaz felt about Wander Canyon Ranch. "I don't see how you can say that."

"Oh, Chaz thinks he needs Wander. Thinks he can't ever belong anywhere else. Mostly because he didn't have anywhere to belong until he got here. When I married Mariah, Chaz's mother, I gave him the choice of keeping his last name or changing it to ours."

Given that Chaz introduced himself as Chaz Walker, it was clear which choice he'd made. "I don't see your point."

"The point is that boy took my last name on so fast it was like grabbing on to a life ring in a flood." He made it sound like welcoming Hank as a father figure in his young life was some kind of weakness. "Clung to it," Hank went on. "Hid under it. Still does."

"So this is some sort of pushing him out of the nest?" Suddenly Yvonne could see a glimpse of the demanding father Chaz had described. Yvonne rose from her chair. "He's a grown man who has put his life into this ranch. He loves this land. As much as you do, if not more. And you're taking it from him. How can you do that if you care about him?"

"What he is is a grown man who's spent most of his life trying to prove himself to me. He's been so set on being the perfect son that he's forgot to become his own man."

Yvonne walked toward him. "Isn't that on you? You're his father—or the man he sees as his father. He doesn't call you Hank. He calls you Dad. If he feels he has to prove himself to you, it's because you make him feel that. I mean, you've just shown him—in the worst possible way—that he isn't equal to Wyatt in your eyes."

"He isn't equal." Hank's voice rose.

Yvonne's breath caught. She hadn't expected Hank to admit that so directly.

"He's better," Hank said, his voice breaking a bit on the admission.

She stared at Hank, not sure what to do with such a statement.

"Better in some ways, worse in others. I can't treat them equally because they aren't." Hank began pacing the deck, words erupting out of him as if he'd needed to talk to someone about this for a long time— which was probably true.

"Only I can't figure out how to treat them different. In the right way, at least. That's part of what Pauline showed me." He threw his arms up in the air. "They'll just lock horns for the rest of their lives unless I settle this now." His voice faltered a bit as he continued. "I need Pauline. I know this is what I've got to do, but I need her to help me do it right."

Hank banged his hand on the railing. "I don't expect you to understand. I don't know why I thought bringing you out here would help. I've lost Pauline and who knows if I've lost the boys." He pushed open the deck gate, grabbed his hat off the railing post where he had set it and put one foot on the steps that led down into the long shadows stretching dusk across grass. "I'm sorry."

He was right—she didn't really follow his thinking. She still believed he'd made a cruel choice and didn't really understand why the ranch wasn't big enough for both brothers. Some part of her had agreed to come out here so she could prove to herself she shouldn't like Hank. Disliking him made it easier to believe she'd made the right call expressing her doubts to Pauline.

Watching Hank Walker stand in that darkening field, one solitary man in a long wide stretch of pasture, she thought he looked like the loneliest man on the planet.

She realized, at that moment, that he was right about one thing: he couldn't get this right without Pauline.

Maybe love was messy and uncertain and filled with faulty people just trying to figure out the right thing to do. Maybe the whole point of love was to fix broken things.

She was different from her sisters, and all she ever felt was her mother's intolerance of that difference. Equal didn't have to mean identical, but it never worked out that way in her family. Endless comparisons with Janice's and Rita's successes never helped. They never motivated or guided her actions or thinking. At least, not in the way Mama seemed to think they should. They only succeeded in making her feel more different, and that her difference was somehow wrong.

That was what she loved about Auntie P. Her aunt knew how to celebrate the ways she was different. How to love her into finding her own way in the world.

Yvonne sat back down into the seat, a bit stunned at the revelation. Hank really did need Auntie P. They deserved the chance to try to work this out. Not just for them, but for Wyatt and Chaz. In two days she was due to return to Matrimony Valley, so there was really only one thing to do.

*I pray You'll stop this if I'm wrong, Lord,* Yvonne prayed, *but I don't think I am.*

She pulled out her phone, brought up Auntie P.'s name and typed in one word of text: Come.

## Chapter Sixteen

Chaz stood in his moonlit kitchen and stared across the lawn at the darkened windows of the big house. This house had always been his private space, but suddenly it felt far too much like the guesthouse it had once been.

The moon was high overhead—no surprise as it was almost two o'clock in the morning. Wyatt had already pulled in an hour ago from whatever carousing he had done, loud music blasting from the cab of his truck despite the time.

Wyatt's noisy return hadn't woken him up. He'd been awake for hours, wandering around the house all night with Cecil following loyally behind him.

And while ranch problems had been known to keep him up some nights, an entirely different problem robbed him of sleep tonight. The image of Yvonne Niles, laughing her head off on a giant carousel grasshopper, light and easy and perfect in his grip as he helped her down and set her far too close, made sleep impossible.

Chaz snapped on the kitchen light, hoping the brightness would stop his brain from replaying the sound of her laughter. Yvonne's laugh was a startling balm to him, as musical as the carousel organ's tune, pouring out of her with no effort at all. He remembered the sound so keenly, it echoed almost as a physical sensation under his ribs. As if he'd somehow inhaled her laughter and could hold it forever inside him.

He filled a water glass, shaking his head at the fool notion. That was the kind of thing Dad had started saying about Pauline when all this mess started.

He stopped right in the middle of lifting the glass, struck by the implications of that stray thought. Dad was foolhardy, head-over-heels smitten with Pauline. And here he was, sleepless, feeling the start of I-might-do-anything-to-stay-close-to-her feelings about Yvonne.

He couldn't stop thinking about her. Not only that, he didn't *want* to stop thinking about her. Chaz set down the glass and planted his hands on the counter as if the thought had knocked him over. He liked the hold she seemed to have over him. He was falling for Yvonne Niles. There were a million sensible reasons why that was a really, really bad idea, but none of them seemed to add up to much at the moment. He was here, she belonged there, they had almost nothing in common except the drama of his father and her aunt—a drama that just complicated everything further. Even if he and

Yvonne could somehow make it work—not that he had any idea how that could ever happen—there'd be the whole business of Dad and Pauline to contend with.

He wasn't quite sure how he knew the soft knock at his front door was her rather than Dad or Wyatt or anyone else. He definitely didn't know what to do with the way his pulse leaped as he pulled open the door to see her standing there. It felt as if he'd been gasping and could suddenly take a deep breath. As if all of him—skin, bones, all of it—came alive at the sight of her small and soft in the wedge of light. He was glad Cecil's enthusiastic greeting gave him a few seconds to scramble his composure back into place.

"I told her to come," she said with no more explanation than that.

It was impossible to say if his relief was for Dad or for himself. And if it was for Dad's happiness, or his stubborn, selfish hope that Pauline was the only person who might talk Dad out of his plan.

"I saw your light on," she said as he pulled the door open farther and waved her inside. "I can't sleep."

So she couldn't sleep, either. Was it for the same reasons he was up? What would he do if the answer to that question was yes? Why would he be so disappointed if the answer was no?

"What did Dad say when you told him?" He wanted her to stay, so he moved to the fireplace and threw two more logs on the fire he'd let burn down.

"He doesn't know yet. He walked off the deck into the pastures after he told me how he didn't think he could get you and Wyatt on the right path without her." Her voice wobbled a bit, and he felt that settle inside him right next to her laughter. If that was how Dad felt, he'd never said that to him.

"He loves her," she went on, her voice

breaking further. "I mean really, really loves her. Why did I stop that?"

He told himself to remember that breaking voice, to realize that her tender heart would never survive this mess of a family. She had some of Pauline's strength, but not all of it. "First of all," he reassured her, "you didn't stop that."

"Didn't I?" She ran her hands through her mussy hair. It wasn't fair that he found her mussy hair even more adorable than the neat ponytail she often wore. When had the word *adorable* started showing up in his thoughts so alarmingly often? "Auntie P. wasn't going to call it off until I spoke up."

Chaz pushed out a breath. "I haven't spent a lot of time with Pauline, but it's pretty clear to me that nobody talks that woman into anything she isn't of a mind to do." *Rather like her niece*, he thought. "To quote a certain baker I know, it was never really your call."

"Very funny. But what if love's not

enough? I mean, he sat there and told me how much he loves and admires you, and look what he's doing to you. Couldn't he love Pauline and hurt her just as badly?"

He turned from his task at the fireplace, surprised by her words. "He what?"

"I decided to ask him outright why he's handing down the ranch the way he is. He told me, and I still don't quite get it, except that he thinks he can't get it right without Pauline. And he's right. He needs her, which means you need her, and probably Wyatt needs her, so I told her to come. They've got to give this another shot."

*He loves and admires you. You need her, so I told her to come.* Chaz was still tripping over Yvonne's words but asked a different question. "Tell me that again?"

She furrowed her brows at him. "Hasn't he explained it to you?"

Not in any way that made sense to him, and quite frankly, Chaz was suspicious Hank would say just about anything to convince Yvonne right now. "He's given reasons—none that I like. What did he say to you?"

Yvonne curled up on the chair closest to the fireplace, taking a woven blanket that had been Mom's and wrapping it around herself. He noticed how her delicate toes peeked out from in between the fringe. How was it he could find her so strong and yet so delicate at the same time? Everything he felt about this woman seemed to defy reason. "He said the short answer was that Wyatt needs the ranch and you don't."

He'd heard some version of that, and it only served to make his blood boil. He didn't need Wander? Maybe like he didn't need to breathe. *How can Dad not see what this land means to me?* So Dad's nod to his strengths was to punish him? Deprive him of the Walker birthright he thought he'd earned? Chaz merely grunted, not wanting to give voice to the harshness of his thoughts in front of her.

"He loves you, Chaz. I know you can't see that right now, but he does. He told me you were the better man."

Chaz raised an eyebrow at that. Sure, the words struck a deep chord, but he didn't trust the motivation. Dad might say whatever he thought would get him what he wanted right now.

"Okay, maybe not the fairest thing to say when you've got two sons—but that's what he said. And that you needed to make your own life, out from under your need for his approval."

*My need for his approval.* What son didn't need his father's approval? Yvonne flinched at his expression, and he chided himself for not keeping the fire in his gut from showing up in his eyes. Maybe the one thing he could do in this whole mess was make sure she didn't get hurt by it.

Her expression grew intense and earnest, and for a moment he let himself believe she truly cared. "He's gonna do it, Chaz. He believes it's the right thing to do. He just can't figure out how to make you understand."

Because there was no understanding what Dad was doing. And that was Dad—don't bother to understand someone else's point of view, just force the other person to bend to yours. She was right about one thing: he was gonna do it. Pauline might be coming, and she might find some ways to smooth things over, but she had no more chance of stopping this succession plan than he did.

"Imagine that." He poked the fire hard and the burst of flames that brightened the room mirrored the searing he felt in his gut. "My stepfather can't figure out how to make me understand the finer points of yanking my future out from underneath me while he paves a nice smooth road for his boy. But I should be the bigger man and swallow it for my own good, huh? That's rich."

"Chaz…"

Right there was the one thing that undid him—the way she said his name. There was so much care in it—too much. How did she manage to say his name with such importance? In a way that made him want to be important to someone…to anyone.

To her.

He stared at her, willing her to say his name again in that tone, with that care. He wanted to hear her say his name like he was the most important person in the world to her. Because whether he liked it or not, she was becoming the most important person in the world to him.

Chaz was one giant, angry ball of pain. Yvonne felt as if she were quite possibly looking at the loneliest heart she'd ever seen. So much pain. So sure he didn't matter. The way her heart ached for his isolation took her breath away.

"He loves you, Chaz." It was an intrusive, personal thing to say to someone she'd known so short a time. But she knew it to be true. "Can you see that? At all?"

She could see him push it away, trying to stop it from sinking in. Trying to keep up the wall he'd raised around himself.

"Has he ever told you?" she pressed. "Really told you that he loves you?"

"He took me and Mom in. Gave us a life." He grabbed at the words like the life raft Hank had spoken of, and at the same time she could see how they stung.

"That's not the same thing. And it's not what I asked." She rose up off the couch, and a look of panic flashed through his eyes. As if he might run from the room if she got closer. As if he was holding that wall up with the last ounce of his will.

There was something deeply loyal about him. Hank may have stepped on it, but he didn't stomp it out. There was a certainty between her and Chaz that she'd never felt with Neal. He had none of Neal's grandiose charm. As a matter of fact, he resented Wyatt's dose of that charm when it was turned on her for even a second. But Chaz didn't need charm. What he had went deeper than that. When that man chose to give his heart, it would be a solid, unshakable thing.

She wanted that. She wanted Chaz's fierce and cautious heart to wrap itself solid and unshakable around her. To have him give her the protection and care she'd seen him give to Cecil, and this land, and even his stepfather. She hadn't even realized how much she wanted it until just this moment, when the pain in his eyes pried loose the door Neal had slammed shut with the back of his hand.

*He would never hurt me.* How long had it been since she could say that about someone? "When's the last time he told you he cares about you?" She could barely force the words out for all the emotion behind them.

He swallowed hard, his hand on the fireplace mantel as if it were the only thing on earth holding him upright.

"When's the last time anyone told you they cared about you? Not needed you or respected you or depended on you, but cared about you?"

He didn't answer. And yet he did—his whole body, the way the fire reflected in his eyes, the way he stood there as if he'd been holding himself up alone for too many years. So much strength. So much solitude. Too much of both to let the rest of the world inside. No wonder a place of light and hope and ease like Matrimony Valley baffled him.

She reached for the fireplace poker still in his hand, white-knuckled in his grip as if it was his last defense to letting her in. She slipped it from his hand, placing it carefully back in the rack beside the now-roaring fire.

Yvonne looked up at him. The flames cut sharp, dancing shadows across his chin and brow. His eyes held fear, disbelief, care, hurt—a thousand things all at once. *Let me in. Let me care. Because I do.* Maybe they really were just two broken people trying to pull something good out of a mess.

There was something exquisite in the fact that she had to stand up on her tiptoes to leave a soft kiss on his cheek. Actually, to call it *soft* was a mistake. It was a small, sparkling, feisty declaration that the impossible-feeling thing between them was real. More quietly real than anything shouted from Matrimony Valley's romantic rooftops.

She heard his breath catch at the contact. He put one hand on her shoulder and held her back a bit. She couldn't say if he was trying to stop himself or her—both were impossible now. His eyes burned with longing and uncertainty, as if to say "Are you sure?"

She was. Mess and all, she was sure. The glow that started in the depth of her heart radiated out to her smile with no need of words. Yvonne held his gaze and nodded just a bit. Chaz Walker was a handsome man, but she could never remember a man looking more *true* to her. What a gift that was.

Chaz ran the backs of his fingers over the curve of her cheek, as if he needed reassurance she was really there. And then he pulled her into his arms—oh, the strength of those arms. She'd felt glimpses of it earlier, but now they fully encircled her, literally sweeping her off her feet. He kissed her tenderly, as though she were the most precious thing in all the world. And then he kissed her fiercely, as if he enthralled her beyond reason, as if he would defend her with his last breath.

Yvonne let herself fall spinning into the sensation of his embrace, into the power of his kiss. She reveled in this amazing thing they'd both resisted and neither expected. She hadn't even realized how much of her heart she'd shut down until Chaz's kiss brought it roaring back to life.

He took her face in his hands when he finally pulled away, a puzzled wonderment in his eyes that almost made her laugh. She felt light and sparkling enough to throw her head back and laugh, and then again she felt soft and quiet and settled.

He grinned. A grin quite different from the sly half smiles he'd shown before. This one was warm and full, extending all the way to the glow in his eyes. "I guess it doesn't skip a generation."

It took her a minute to work out what he meant. "You mean like Hank and Pauline? She's my aunt, not my mother."

He laughed. "And he's not technically my father. But it kind of feels like we inherited this from them, doesn't it?"

He pulled her close to him, and she discovered she fit perfectly against his chest and under his chin. She closed her eyes as she felt his arms tighten around her. "You're right—it does."

## Chapter Seventeen

Everything had changed. And nothing had changed.

One kiss—actually, it had turned into several before he dutifully walked her back to the big house—seemed to double his need to be near her. Overnight, the sense of her presence had focused to a kind of radar about her. He needed to know where she was—all the time. Not because he was worried about her—she could likely take care of herself—but because he *wanted* to protect her, wanted her close. He found himself continually wondering what she was thinking. Of just about everything. Did she see how glorious the sunrise was this morning? Had she lain awake for hours like he had after they parted last night?

Dad was running around the house in a happy panic this morning, thrilled Pauline was on her way. In true Pauline fashion, she'd booked the first flight out, and Yvonne was taking his vehicle to the airport to pick up Pauline in half an hour. They'd left Dad to his preparations, opting instead to grab time at his favorite bakery. They needed to figure this out, to talk away from Hank and Wyatt, but neither of them seemed to know how to start this totally unexpected conversation.

"Their engagement sure has been a roller coaster." He felt awkward and tongue-tied as he stared at her and she gaped at him. Dad had once used the word *thunderstruck* to describe how he'd felt when he first met Pauline. He definitely felt thunderstruck this morning. He wanted to kiss Yvonne, but it felt much riskier in the clarity of sunlight. He needed to be alone with her, but suddenly didn't know how. He wanted to pull her into a corner and hold her close for hours, anchoring himself to her joy. At the same time, he wanted to run from the out-of-control way he felt around her.

"Sure has," she fumbled back without her usual directness, one hand playing nervously with her hair. From all the emotions playing on her face, she was as unmoored as he was. Now what? That and a dozen other questions—none of which he could spit out—piled up in his brain.

Chaz had an appointment at the land broker's office in twenty minutes, and the prospect of mundane ranch business felt totally beyond him at the moment. How was he supposed to do paperwork when both their worlds just tilted off balance last night?

He was dying to touch her, to hold her hand in the hopes it could somehow ground him in the chaos. Only he couldn't bring himself to be seen looking so love-struck in front of people who knew him.

Which meant...what, exactly?

"These are delicious," Yvonne answered too brightly. She dealt with her nerves by devouring a trio of cupcakes so fast she had a smear of frosting on one cheek.

It was insane how madly he wanted to kiss it off. Instead, he pointed to her cheek. She blushed as she wiped it with a napkin.

Fallen hard and acting stupid. At this moment, it was easy to see why Dad made any number of bad decisions with Pauline in the picture. He couldn't recall a single crucial point for the meeting it had taken two weeks to schedule. He didn't even want to go—had she not asked to pick up Pauline alone so they could talk, he might have canceled just to be with her.

"Hank is so happy she's coming. So it sounds like they're back on again." She seemed to be trying to fill the buzzing, electric air between them with words, but wasn't having any more success than he was. "I'm glad—I think. They seem to be good for each other if they can calm down a bit."

"Dad said he was on the phone for over an hour with Pauline last night. They decided to push the wedding date back. Sounds like a smart plan to me."

He'd talked with Dad this morning, expressed how glad he was that Pauline was coming out to the ranch. But he couldn't bring himself to tell Dad what had happened. Not yet. He definitely had a new appreciation for his stepfather's urgency, however. He wasn't feeling smart this morning, not at all. Some new irrational part of him kept spouting absurd plots to keep Yvonne from getting on a plane back to Matrimony Valley the day after tomorrow.

Yvonne reached out and ran one delicate finger down the back of his hand as it rested on the table. The prospect of her going back to the valley while he stayed here became almost unbearable, igniting a panic he didn't know how to keep in check.

Ruth came over and refilled both of their already full coffee cups. She owned the bakery where they were sitting. Yvonne's attempt to casually pull her hand from Chaz's did not go unnoticed. "Is this the pretty lady Nate told me you took on the carousel yesterday?" Her eyebrows waggled with the question.

Chaz cleared his throat, feeling the color rise up his neck as if he were fifteen. "Ruth, this is Yvonne Niles. She's the niece of Dad's…" He tripped a bit over the word, unsure if it was officially back in place yet. "…fiancée. Yvonne runs a bakery back in North Carolina, where Pauline's from." Maybe if they could talk shop, it'd keep Ruth from the meddling she clearly had planned.

Ruth nodded toward Yvonne. "Hank tells me it's a wedding town. How's that work?"

Yvonne launched into the safe conversation topic. "We're a venue for rustic destination weddings. I do the cakes, someone else does the flowers, my friend Hailey runs the inn, and we have a very pretty waterfall."

"Yvonne makes a special German chocolate wedding cake that's famous in those parts."

Ruth leaned back on one hip. "German chocolate, huh? White or dark icing?"

Yvonne's gaze shifted between Ruth and Chaz, as if she'd been just as surprised by Chaz's comment as he was. "Both, actually. Bride's choice. And groom's," she added after a second, remembering their first conversation in the same instant he did.

Ruth exhaled. "I've been baking in Wander Canyon for forty-two years. Pies are my thing, but everybody seems to want cakes and cupcakes lately. I do wedding cakes, but not as much anymore. I'm ready to slow down a bit, and weddings are a lot of work."

"You can say that again," Yvonne commiserated. "But you make a mean cupcake. These were all delicious."

"Imagine that," Ruth said. Her tone wasn't talking about the *what* Yvonne had eaten, but about *when* and *with whom*. Wander Canyon could rival Matrimony Valley in gossip and meddling. There was little hope of hiding anything now.

"You can't slow down, Ruth," Chaz said, trying to make conversation. "Where'll I get my cookies?"

"I'm not the only woman who can make a decent oatmeal raisin cookie." Ruth looked straight at Yvonne with that comment. "But I'll make sure to pass on my recipe to whoever buys the shop."

"You're selling?" Chaz hadn't heard that news.

"I'm thinking about it. Sixty-three is too old to get up so early every morning. My knees aren't ready to face the world until well after eight these days."

"Have you got a buyer lined up?" Yvonne asked.

"Not yet," Ruth said. Chaz wished she

didn't get such an insinuating look on her face when she added, "But I'm hopeful the right person will come along."

Ruth was selling the bakery. Yvonne wanted a new start somewhere outside the valley. It couldn't possibly be that easy, could it?

*Do you really think you can uproot her life on your account?* a dark voice whispered in the back of his mind. *Besides, what have you got to offer her? Not Wander Canyon Ranch. Not anymore.*

He checked his watch and handed her the keys to his truck. "You'd better get going—Pauline lands in forty minutes."

She took the keys from him, eyes narrowing as if she could hear his doubts. "Wyatt'll fetch me home after my meeting and we can..." What? He didn't know the next step on any front. "...take it from there," he finished, feeling lost and insufficient.

Yvonne stood, paused for a moment and then leaned down and kissed his cheek in a gesture so profoundly gentle he lost his breath. "I'll be back soon."

He knew, at that moment, that he never wanted her to leave. He just didn't know if what he wanted ever got to matter.

Yvonne pulled the truck up to the airport sidewalk where Pauline stood waving hello. "You sure hopped that plane fast," she said as she hoisted Auntie P.'s suitcase into the cab's small back seat.

Pauline pursed her lips. "I may or may not have had a flight already picked out."

Yvonne felt her jaw drop. "You were already coming out?"

"Let's just say I was thinking and praying on it." Her bright eyes softened. "Mercy, but I miss that man."

"He sure misses you." She gave her aunt a quick look before they pulled out onto the highway. "That man is full out one hundred percent in love with you." She felt obliged to add, "But you'll be smart about things, won't you?"

Pauline gave a sudden laugh and shook her head.

"What?" Yvonne asked. "I want what's best for you."

"I'm just thinking about what your youth pastor used to say."

Yvonne began to laugh, as well. Together they recited the man's favorite words of wisdom: "If you're going to do something stupid, at least be smart about it."

"We're not teenagers, Yvonne. If I head into this, it'll be with my eyes wide open. I'm still not happy with his plans, but what you said about him needing help to do right by them made sense. He said much the same thing when he called me yesterday. I just wish we could have had that whole conversation before he came to the valley. So I guess we're learning as we go."

Yvonne could only smile at the look in Hank's eyes this morning. He'd said thank you about two dozen times, even pulling her in a giant hug. The man looked as if she'd given him his life back. Maybe in some ways she had—or at least another shot at happiness.

But what about her happiness? Did that include Chaz? Last night it had seemed inevitable and wildly romantic. Her mind recalled the tremendous sense of peace she felt in his arms. The way he could look into her eyes and see all her feelings. The way his arms felt as if they could hold her close and upright in the fiercest storm. She'd never felt anything like that in her life, even with Neal. Neal's affections always felt as if they had to be earned somehow, whereas she instantly knew Chaz's were freely given and steadfast.

This morning felt anything but steadfast. This morning reality clamored up against last night's peace. Their fumbled conversation in the bakery sprouted doubts that the feelings had come too hard and too fast to be trusted. Hank and Pauline seemed ready to shout their love from the rooftops—what did it say that neither she nor Chaz was ready to reveal their feelings to anyone else just yet?

And still that one word kept coming to mind. *Steadfast.* Was it real? Would it last? Could the powerful pull she felt toward Chaz be the beginnings of real, deep love?

She turned onto the exit marked for the route to Wander Canyon and noticed Pauline was staring at her.

"All right, Yvonne. Out with it."

Of course she felt completely different since Chaz had kissed her, but she didn't think it showed. Then again, this was Auntie P.

"With what?"

Pauline crossed her arms over her chest. "You know better than to try that with me. What's going on?"

Yvonne had no hope of hiding it, even though she couldn't bear for anyone to know. Her heart seemed to pound with impossible and wrong and silly and absolutely right feelings all at the same time. She was falling hard and fast, with little hope of denying it. "It's more of a 'who' than a 'what,'" she admitted.

"Hank?"

"No, not Hank. He's been very nice, actually."

"Wyatt's not up to his usual tricks, is he?" Yvonne could hear from Pauline's tone that she already knew it was neither Hank nor Wyatt.

"No, although it's easy to see why Wyatt and his brother are at each other's throats all the time." She avoided saying Chaz's name, which felt absurd. "They couldn't be more different."

Pauline gave a small *aha* hum before asking, "Well, then, who's the 'who'?"

Yvonne kept her eyes glued to the road and ignored the flush that seemed to run through her as she blurted out "Chaz."

Auntie P. was quiet for a moment. "Chaz," she said, the one syllable infused with a dozen tones. "Chaz," she repeated, and Yvonne knew her secret was out. "As in you and Chaz."

It was startling to hear someone else say it. The kisses had been real enough, but it was something private and wondrous between them. A jolt of panic that now someone else knew—even if that someone was Auntie P.—made her breath shorten up.

"Well, it took you two long enough."

Yvonne nearly drove off the road. "What?"

"I've known you two were perfect for each other since I met him. You don't think we actually needed that man's help for the wedding, do you?"

Yvonne pulled to the side of the road and slammed the truck into Park. "Are you saying you brought Chaz to Matrimony Valley to meet me?" Granted, both Matrimony Valley and Auntie P. were famous for the extent of their meddling, but this was a shade too far, even for them.

Yvonne was relieved when Pauline said, "Well, no. It wasn't as deliberate as that."

"I'm glad to hear that."

"I meant it when I told you I didn't realize Hank was planning to do what he did. But you were one of the reasons I thought it was a good idea for Chaz to come along when Hank suggested it."

Yvonne tried to wrap her mind around Auntie P.'s words. "You set me up with your future son-in-law?"

Pauline balked. "I wouldn't go so far as to say that. I like to think I just held the door open for the possibility. But that night, at the car accident, I saw something. You would be good for him—and he for you."

She said it so matter-of-factly. But facts didn't come into this at all. Yvonne wasn't even seeing how logic came into it at the moment. "It's not like a recipe. You don't just throw people together like ingredients and get…cake."

"Someone from Matrimony Valley, of all places, ought to see it with a bit more optimism than that. And don't tell me you don't see it. It's all over your face, hon, although you're trying very hard to hide it. I'll see the same thing when I set my eyes on him, won't I?"

There seemed little point in arguing what they both knew to be true. Yvonne ran her hands through her hair. "I hardly know him."

That brought a laugh from Pauline. "Well, I'm hardly one to talk about the cautions of a whirlwind romance, am I? You know, Hank told me he saw something that night, too, which tells me it must have been clear as day."

"Well, I didn't see it. Then."

"You never see it yourself. At least not at first. But tell me, did you know Kelly and

Bruce belonged together before either of them would admit it?"

Auntie P. could be so aggravating when she was right. "Maybe."

"And what about Jean and Josh. Could you see that one coming?"

This was spiraling out of her control. "Auntie P., that's not how this works."

Pauline smiled. "Darlin', that's almost always how this works." Her aunt put her hand gently on her arm. "Just what is it you're afraid of?"

It didn't take much thought to come up with the answer. Her heart had been groaning it since the night Chaz took her into his arms. It was putting those feelings into words that stumped her. "That... I'm wrong about him. That he'll turn out to hurt me." A surprising threat of tears welled up out of nowhere, choking any further words.

"After all," Pauline finished for her, "you turned out to be wrong about Neal, and he hurt you. Literally." Pauline squeezed her arm. "I am so sorry for that. I wish every day that one of us had seen it earlier, but I also thank God you hadn't yet married that man."

Yvonne simply nodded, gulping out a weak "Me, too."

"It's a shame, absolutely. But don't you think the bigger shame would be if you let that rob you of something that might be wonderful?"

"How will I know?" The question came out of her with a yelp.

"That's just it," Pauline replied. "You don't."

# Chapter Eighteen

For an hour or two, there was a splendid peace on Wander Canyon Ranch. Hank and Pauline's reunion was sweet—if tentative. It warmed Yvonne's heart to watch them cautiously hold hands and talk in low, tender tones about how much they had missed each other. It was clear to her how in love they were, and how hard they were both willing to work together to make their future happen. *He's right*, Yvonne thought as she saw Hank cherish her presence on the ranch. *The only way he can hope to make this work is with her beside him. They need each other. That's how it's supposed to be, isn't it?* Neal had taught her to be frightened of needing someone like that. But Chaz wasn't Neal—he wasn't anything like Neal. She could need Chaz and be safe. *Oh, Lord, am I ready to believe that? Is that why You brought me here? Or is it why I'm going home?*

Yvonne's thoughts tumbled around her as she moved her things out of what Hank had called Pauline's room. Her aunt's happy reunion only served to rise up new doubts for herself. It wasn't the logistics of sleeping in a new room for her last night on the ranch. That was no bother at all. It was what came—or didn't come—next. What happened after she stepped onto that plane back to Matrimony Valley tomorrow?

On the one hand, it was becoming clear that she'd get to bake for Hank and Pauline's back-on-again wedding. Maybe not on the original rushed timetable, but wasn't that for the best anyway? *I believe You'll see them through, Lord*, she prayed as she set her things down in another guest room. *Maybe You knew they had to go through this bump in order to move forward.*

*But which direction is forward for me?*

She couldn't deny she was drawn to this place. Something about the fresh crisp air spoke of new beginnings to her. And Pauline would be relocated out here once she married Hank. Surely it was no coincidence that charming bakery in town was in the market for a new owner. All these things spoke of one possible path for her future. Cathy had even emailed her several times to say she was doing well managing Bliss Bakery. Perhaps she was even ready to buy the business if Yvonne chose to sell. Move?

Or not. Or at least, not yet. A big piece of that caution belonged to Chaz. Where once she'd wondered if she could ever stop arguing with that man, now she wondered if she could ever stop thinking about him. The thing between them was strong. Her pull toward the canyon and toward Chaz had risen up so fast and so powerful that, to be honest, it frightened her. She had never been able to take Pauline's drastic leaps through life, and now was no time to start. *I don't really know him,* she told herself even as she looked out the window to see if he had returned with Wyatt yet. *Certainly not enough to uproot myself. I was so sure— and so wrong—about Neal. I couldn't live with being wrong again.*

*So what do I do now?* Could they pursue whatever this was from a distance? Would taking some time give Chaz the chance to iron things out with Hank and Wyatt? If it was true and strong, a little time wouldn't dilute the care growing between them. After all, they had built-in opportunities to see each other as Hank and Pauline's wedding plans progressed.

It reminded her of Pauline's admission that both she and Hank had seen the connection long before she had herself. She'd seen Jean's love for Josh before the couple figured it out for themselves. She'd sensed the attraction between Kelly and Bruce early on, as well. Could it be the same for...?

"Hank!"

She heard Pauline's voice through the open window beside her, saw her aunt rush out onto the deck in search of Hank.

"Hank!" Pauline was shouting as she dashed back inside the house. "Come quick!"

Yvonne made her way quickly down the stairs as Hank came inside from the side door. "What?"

"In the barn," Pauline said breathlessly as she tugged on Hank's arm. "They look like they're gonna kill each other."

"Who?"

Pauline rolled her eyes in exasperation. "Chaz and Wyatt. They're in the barn throwing punches at each other. I heard the shouting. You've got to go stop them!"

As the three of them ran out the door in the direction of the barn, Yvonne realized the brothers should have been back at least an hour ago. She caught sight of Wyatt's truck parked outside the barn but couldn't say how long it had been there. Even before they were close to the doors, Yvonne could hear shouts. Pounding sounds filled the air, as well as the crash and splinter of things falling over. Pauline was right; it did sound as if they would kill each other.

Hank pushed through the door with the force of a father who'd broken up more than his share of fights. "Stand down, you two!" he bellowed even before they were inside.

"Oh, my!" Pauline gasped as they turned the corner past the stalls to find Chaz and Wyatt tangled in a bloody, dirty tumble of straw, arms and legs on the barn floor.

It was as if they didn't even hear Hank. They rolled over several times until Wyatt reeled back and sent a blow to Chaz's shoulder. Chaz growled and tossed Wyatt off hard enough to hit a nearby trunk. Then he staggered up to lunge at his brother again.

Hank grabbed a rake beside him and banged it so hard against the barn wall that the whole room shook. "Stop!" he yelled at the top of his voice.

The men startled at the sound, turning toward Hank even as their chests heaved from the battle. From the look of it, they'd been at it for a while. Both men were winded and bloody, each backing away to slump against opposite walls even as they traded angry glares.

Hank stormed into the center of the room, planting himself between them. "What is going on?"

Neither man answered. Wyatt brushed the straw out of his hair while Chaz wiped the blood from his chin with the back of his hand. They'd have a pair of shiners—if not more—between the two of them based on the swollen squint of their eyes. Wyatt had a scrape down the side of his neck. One sleeve on Chaz's shirt hung ripped from the shoulder.

"What do you think is going on?" Chaz finally ground out. Yvonne tried to catch his gaze but the man's temper was too far gone. Rage from the two brothers seemed to fill the huge room.

Hank walked a slow arc between them. "Decided to settle this by beating each other to pieces, did you?"

"It's not my doing," Wyatt sneered.

"It's *never* your doing, is it?" Chaz snarled right back.

"Maybe we'd better leave," Pauline said quietly as she grabbed Yvonne's arm.

"Don't," Chaz barked out. "You need to stay. I want you to hear. I want all of you to hear what Wyatt just told me."

"Still running to Dad to tattle, are you?" Wyatt spit out blood with the words.

It looked to Yvonne as if Chaz was rattling with rage. What would have happened if Pauline had not seen them?

"How about you grow a spine and say it to him instead of me, then?" Chaz's eyes were cold and hard. "Or does that take too much effort, *brother*?" He flung the title at Wyatt like a spear.

Wyatt's gaze flicked back and forth between Hank and Chaz.

"What is it, son?" Hank's words were low and sharply edged.

"Son," Chaz echoed bitterly, turning from his stepbrother and stepfather as if the word had pushed him against the wall. When Wyatt said nothing, Chaz suddenly wheeled around and rushed Wyatt, growling, "I want them all to hear it from you, you ungrateful…"

"Stop now!" Hank's booming voice filled the room again, grinding Chaz to a halt. Hank spread his hands between the men, taking two deep breaths as Chaz retreated back to the wall. "Hear what?" Hank asked.

Wyatt's breaths came harder, and he ran his hands through his hair as he began to pace his side of the room. Pauline and Yvonne looked at each other, feeling the tension crackle between the three men. Chaz looked as if he'd give Wyatt only a handful of seconds before the fight started up again. If that happened, Yvonne wondered if even Hank could stop them.

"I don't want it," Wyatt said through gritted teeth.

The whole room—the whole world—ground to a stop.

"I don't want the ranch," Wyatt said louder. "I never did."

Yvonne felt Pauline's hand tighten on hers.

Hank stared at Wyatt. "What are you saying?"

Wyatt gave a dark laugh. "What am I saying? You know what I just said. Only you can't hear it. I've been trying to tell you for years, but you never could hear it." He walked right up to stand toe to toe with his father. "How about if I shout it at you, Dad? Will that help?" He raised his hands practically in Hank's face, shouting each word. "I don't want the ranch! Loud and clear yet?"

Wyatt could not have struck his father with more force had he thrown a punch. Yvonne's chest tightened at the wounds in Hank's eyes, and she heard Pauline gasp beside her. And Chaz—Chaz had bitter anger igniting behind his eyes. The entire canyon didn't seem large enough to hold the surge of anger and hurt boiling in front of her.

"I'm going to pretend I didn't hear that come out of your ungrateful mouth," Hank ground out, his fingers clenched into white-knuckled fists.

"Sure. Go on, pretend. It's what you've always done, isn't it?" Wyatt snarled. "How could I ever want something different from what you want?"

"This is your land." Hank spoke it with the air of law.

"No, Dad, this is your land. It's not...in me like that."

Without warning, Chaz made a low snarling sound and stormed past the four of them and out the barn door. He turned immediately toward the pastures, as if he couldn't bear to keep the house in sight.

It had taken only a fraction of a second to see the crush of unfairness descend on Chaz's features. Yvonne went to follow him, but Pauline held her back, shaking her head. "He can't hear anything you have to say right now."

"But…" Her own heart stung. Chaz must feel as if his had been hollowed out and burned.

"Give that man space. Pray—hard—but best give him space."

The two of them turned back to the remaining men. Hank's eyes were narrow and riveted on Wyatt. "Pauline, honey," he said without looking, "take Yvonne and go back to the house."

Yvonne expected Pauline to push back against a command like that, especially given the anger boiling between the father and son in front of her, but Pauline said nothing. She only kept hold of Yvonne's hand and walked out of the barn in the opposite direction Chaz had taken, back toward the house she had hoped to soon call home.

Twelve canyons weren't big enough to hold the storm inside him. Chaz walked, and then ran until his lungs burned, and then kept walking until the dusk swallowed him, dark as his mood.

*I get nothing.* The words drummed through him over and over. *Nothing. Cast-offs. Leftovers.* What was that Bible verse about even the dogs eating crumbs from the rich man's table?

A reasonable man might say he should be happy with Wyatt's unfathomable rejection of Wander Canyon Ranch. After all, if Wyatt didn't want it, Dad could only choose to give it to him, right?

Only Chaz couldn't come anywhere near

reason about this. Wyatt's idiocy had tainted Wander as crumbs, a leftover discarded by the true blood heir. It was as if every second-best rating Chaz had ever choked down came rushing back to drown him. The world had never handed him anything without a fight, never granted him first place in anything. Why think that could ever change? Some people got a feast of a life. Others would always be doomed to fight for the scraps.

His mistake had been to dare to want it so badly. He'd let himself believe that he belonged. That his place in the family went deeper than the Walker name and the years of trying to please.

*He said you're the better man, the stronger man.* There wasn't a single thing Yvonne could have said to him that would have cut deeper than that.

Yvonne. She'd woken up some part of him that had shut down and stopped trying. The way she looked at him, the way she viewed him as loyal and worthwhile, it made it all worse. He'd gone through life with clenched fists, fighting and clawing to belong. She'd made him think it could be different. That love could be given rather than earned. Wasn't that what her faith— the faith he'd once had but that had withered until her nosy, gutsy care had managed to nudge it awake again—was all about?

More than his soul, more than his heart, the hardest thing was this: he'd started to believe he really might be the man she saw in him.

He'd wanted the ranch—and not even all to himself, just in equal measure—for as long as he could remember. Now, even if he got it, he wasn't sure he could ever get past the sour taste of having received it because Wyatt didn't want it.

*Why did You even bother, Lord?* Not very noble a thought for the first prayer he'd said in a long time. *I can't bear to stay. I can't bear to leave. I can barely stand to exist at the moment.* Wander would be a storm of

hurt and anger and broken family now—
one even Pauline couldn't hope to fix it anytime soon.

*Yvonne deserves better. Grant me enough
strength to let her go to someone who is.*

His mistake was ever daring to think he
deserved someone like her in the first place.

Yvonne put another log on the fire and
wrapped the thick blanket around herself.
Even with Cecil at her feet, Chaz's house
was full of shadows and echoes, empty instead of spacious.

He'd been gone for hours. The night had
grown cold and he'd had no coat when
he stormed off earlier that afternoon. His
truck was still here, so he had to be on foot,
wherever he was. Her brain kept painting
pictures of him yelling in the mountains,
throwing huge rocks down ravines the way
he'd hurled stones in the river back in the
valley. There weren't big-enough rocks for
what had happened this afternoon.

Hank hadn't said a word since he returned

from the barn about a half an hour after she'd left with Pauline. Wyatt's truck tires had squealed out of the driveway a few minutes after Hank had come through the door.

When Hank went up the stairs and slammed the bedroom door shut, Pauline did not go after him. Her aunt, unafraid to tackle most any problem, looked afraid to tackle this. Yvonne didn't blame her one bit.

*Lord,* she cried in her heart as she listened in the darkness for the latch of Chaz's door, *what are You doing? Why all this pain?* She couldn't think of an outcome that caused more hurt all around. Hank hadn't strengthened Chaz; he'd broken him.

She dozed, sad and cold, until footsteps woke her. The man who stood over her bore little resemblance to the man she'd kissed in front of this fireplace just last night.

"Go home," he said, his words flat and lifeless.

"I wanted to make sure you were okay," she said, rising. She reached for his hand, but he pulled it away. "I'll go back to the big house once I know you're all right."

"All right?" He echoed her words with a dark and hollow laugh that sent goose bumps down her arms. "I don't think so."

She asked the only question there was right now. "Will you accept it? The ranch?"

He turned away from her. "What do you care?"

She'd always thought the most painful sting in her life had come from Neal's hand, but she was wrong. "I know it's not how you wanted it, but…"

"Go home," he growled over her words, still refusing to face her. "Go back to your happy little valley where everyone gets the fairy-tale ending. We're fresh out of those here."

"Chaz…"

"Don't," he yelled for a moment. Then she could see his fists clench as he wrestled his seething temper back under control. "Please, don't."

She was not going to leave him to his temper, leave him to lash out in a way that might destroy his dream forever. It was dented, it was surrounded by poor choices and human mistakes, but it wasn't gone. "Are you the better man? Are you strong enough to take the high road here? To reach for what's been placed in front of you?"

"Nothing gets handed to me. Never has." She wasn't even sure he was hearing her words.

Well, she would make him hear. She walked over into his view, and when he turned away she walked into his view again. "It hurts. I get it. And I know you wanted your father to…"

"Stepfather," he corrected.

"Your *dad*," she insisted, "to give you the ranch, or share it, or whatever. And now it looks like it will happen that way, only your stubborn pride won't let you accept it. Are you going to walk away from the thing you love most in the world just because it didn't come to you on your terms?"

He didn't reply. He didn't look at her, but he didn't turn away, either.

She pressed on. "I'm no fan of the way you beat each other up, but I'll give you one thing. You forced the truth to come out. You thought you were fighting Wyatt, but I think you were fighting for Wander. Fighting for Hank to see what he wouldn't see."

"That's rather putting a shine on it, don't you think?"

"No, I don't think. Not at all." She ducked her head down until she could see his downcast eyes. "This is Wander Canyon Ranch, Chaz. The land that's in your blood whether you admit it or not. That's not a castoff. If Hank gives you Wander—and I believe with all my heart that he will—it's because you fought for it and earned it. Not because Wyatt left it behind."

She tried not to let his grunt annoy her. She grabbed his hand, grateful when he didn't pull it away this time. "The man who picked up a wounded dog off the side of the road and turned him into Cecil can accept Wander. Any way it comes to him. And turn it into his future. I believe that. The question is, do you?"

He met her eyes for the first time in what felt like forever, but there was no warmth there. Only cold, hard bitterness. He pulled his hand from hers, and she felt the whole world slip away with his fingers. "No." The house seemed to darken with the finality of the single word. He walked toward the door and opened it without looking at her. "Go home, Yvonne. There's nothing for you here."

## Chapter Nineteen

Yvonne had spent countless hours over the past months asking God to let her heart fill itself with happiness for Pauline. Now Auntie P.'s perfect day was here. In a matter of minutes, she'd become Hank Walker's wife. It was the happy ending every Matrimony Valley resident wished for. The ceremony was set to be beautiful.

The ceremony was missing someone.

Pauline told Yvonne that Chaz left Wander Ranch before her flight back to Matrimony Valley that last morning, and had stayed away. He returned half a month later, resuming his duties to run the ranch, but had done so lifelessly. Efficient, but passionless.

And he was not here.

Wyatt was here instead, standing up as best man where Chaz had once been slated to serve. He was as much Hank's son as Chaz—more so, if you took biology into account—but it still struck Yvonne as sad and wrong. No one talked about Chaz's absence. Everyone took careful pains to be happy and busy, but to Yvonne the hole in the family gaped like the hole in her heart. Try as she might, Yvonne felt Chaz's wounds as if they were her own. They were, in some ways, because his wounds kept him from welcoming her heart.

Was Chaz Walker the steadfast man she saw under all that hurt and pride? Or had she been as wrong about Chaz as she had been about Neal? The answer to that question had not yet come, so she could only wait. She prayed to be like Pauline, who seemed to take the unhealed family wound in bittersweet stride. Pauline kept saying that some things—and some people—took more time than anyone wanted. *How true.*

Yvonne drew her focus back to the happy present as she helped Pauline fix the veil on her hat. The small, smart hat gave a vintage panache to her aunt's elegant white wedding suit. "You look fabulous. I'm so glad you got your happy ending, Auntie P."

"I'm just sorry you didn't get yours yet." Pauline kissed her cheek. "Just you wait. When the road is long and rocky, the final bend is that much sweeter. I'm hoping that final bend is…well…just around the bend. Are you ready, bridesmaid? 'Cause I sure am."

Yvonne picked up her bouquet and turned toward the archway that led into the sanctuary. "Let's go get you married to Hank," she said over the lump in her throat. "That's the happy ending I want to see today."

Pauline's eyes glowed at the sight of her groom. But it was Yvonne's eyes that popped wide open when Pauline pointed with a conspiratorial joy to the man who came out of the sanctuary side room door behind Hank Walker.

Chaz stood next to his father, looking as nervous as the groom himself.

Yvonne turned back to Pauline, who only grinned. Wyatt was also clearly in on the plot. He caught Yvonne's eyes, gave a shrug and made a show of stepping aside to make room for his stepbrother.

What? How? There was no chance to ask what had dissolved the animosity between the two Walker boys. Had they reconciled? Or just put differences aside for the sake of their father today?

"Did you know?" Yvonne whispered as the organ began to play.

"Maybe. Today just got really interesting," Pauline said, waving Yvonne on as if she was late starting down the aisle.

Yvonne laughed and tried to steady herself. "Today had no hope of being anything but interesting."

As she made her way to the end of the aisle and turned for the bridal march, Yvonne tried to read Chaz's expression. She couldn't. She'd have to wait until after the ceremony to even come close to untangling the mystery of how Chaz Walker came to stand in Matrimony Valley Community Church on this crisp December morning.

"Love in spite of everything is my favorite kind of love," Pastor Mitchell began. "It's what our valley does best, I believe. It's what we celebrate today."

This day was for Hank and Pauline, surely, but now her own heart was pounding with the possibility that it might mark a new beginning for her and Chaz, as well. The dark cloud she had seen in his eyes that night seemed to be gone. He had a quietness about him—a peace perhaps?—that cast his features in a new light. She felt her own heart lighten and expand just being in the same room with him. Well, with him and about a hundred and fifty other people, but who was counting?

Yvonne forced her focus back to the ceremony at hand. "Every once in a while," the pastor went on, "it seems our Lord takes His time crafting two hearts for each other." He smiled at Hank and Pauline. "And the wait seems long. And often tangled. But the perfection we see today tells us that God knows exactly what He's doing, even when we can't see it."

Did she dare hope the words suited her and Chaz as much as Hank and Pauline? She'd tried so hard to push Chaz from her heart, but it had never really happened. Chaz chose that moment to meet her gaze, and her breath caught. The connection felt startling and warm, like the moment glowing embers of a fire catch the wind and burst back into flame.

The ceremony seemed to be happening on two levels at once—the wedding of Hank and Pauline everyone was watching and the moments reaching between her and Chaz as they stood beside them. Time both raced by and stood still, the sparkling winter light casting the church's tiny sanctuary in a silvery glow. If God's blessing could be visible, this ceremony certainly looked blessed in all this glorious light.

When Pastor Mitchell smiled broadly and spread his hands, the words "I now pronounce you man and wife" sent up peals of applause from the church pews. Even before the pastor could get the words "You may kiss the bride" out of his mouth, Hank wrapped his arms around his new bride and kissed her. And then kissed her again. She gasped in delight over such a display of romance, and Pauline somehow managed to glow even more. *She's beautiful*, Yvonne thought. And she was. Any young and blushing bride the valley had seen seemed incomparable to the happiness captured in

Hank's and Pauline's eyes as they started back up the aisle.

The moment when Chaz offered his arm, Yvonne lost her battle to squelch the hope. She finally gave in to her persistent optimism that the family had somehow worked its way to restoration. Could Chaz be here for her, as well? Could they inherit the happy ending like they'd inherited the love?

It was love. Or had been. The gaping loss of it had told her that truth. She'd tried to convince herself love really wasn't enough, but it had never taken hold.

"You're here," she gasped as she slipped her hand into his elbow and they started their own procession behind the newlyweds.

"I am," he said. His voice held the glow she'd remembered from the night of their first kiss. Every detail of those moments had been embedded in her memory. Her heart had never really let go. *I love him. Still.*

She felt a bit dizzy from the giddy shock

of it all, grateful to have his steadfast arm to hold. And it *was* there—the steadfastness she'd relished back in Wander. But how? What had transformed him? "But…you… I…" She was sure her mouth was hanging open—hardly a good look for a bridesmaid.

He winked at her—a wink worthy of Pauline, she mused. "Later," he said and led her up the aisle to where a snow shower of white rose petals was dancing in the air over Hank's and Pauline's heads.

Chaz was having fun. Actual, joyful fun. How long had it been?

Yvonne practically yanked him out of the receiving line at the first possible moment, pulling him aside to an alcove in the inn lobby. She lost no time in greeting him with a heart-stopping kiss, but then pressed him for an explanation.

"What happened?"

Chaz had been trying to come up with words to describe the difficult path back to reconciliation with Dad. With Wyatt. With God. Maybe with the whole world. "I woke up," he said. It was the best he could muster, but it wasn't anything close to sufficient. "Some nosy, lovely woman yelled at me about how I was letting my pride keep me from what I'd wanted all along just because it didn't come the way I wanted it." He feathered his fingers against her cheek, feeling like he couldn't stop touching her now that he was back here. "I wouldn't hear those words at first, but eventually they sank in."

"You and Hank? You worked it out? I mean, you must have if you're here."

Chaz took her hand. "I won't say it was easy. Neither of us is quick to own up to our mistakes. But your aunt is pushy." He rolled his eyes. "Relentless, actually."

"God bless Auntie P." A surge of joyful laughter came from the reception, and they both looked in the direction of the party for a moment. She turned back to him, eyes full of questions. "So…?"

They needed a dozen hours to wade through all that had happened, but he tried to tell her anyway. "We found a way through it. I don't know that I'll ever totally get how Dad could choose to give the land to one son over the other. But I did finally understand his motive. Faulty as it was, Dad was sincerely trying to make each of us face up to our shortcomings."

"I told you that's what he said to me. And isn't that what loving fathers are supposed to do?"

He laughed. "Pauline said the exact same thing. And yes, so did you. It just took a couple of thousand tries before it sank in." He moved closer to her. "And I realized, after a long time of sulking, that the only person putting me in second place was me. I can be a bit stubborn, if you haven't noticed."

She bit her lip. "And Wyatt?"

She was asking about every relationship but the one he really wanted to discuss. Chaz reminded himself that if today went the way he planned, he'd have all the time in the world to let Yvonne know what she meant to him.

"That took a little longer. We are brothers, after all. I may never get how Wander doesn't mean as much to him. But I can't fault him for going after what he truly wants. He's been better at it than I was, that's for sure. Dad, too." He gave her a warm smile. "But I'm hoping to change that."

The wonder that had captured his heart returned to her eyes. "Do you? Have what you want?" The breathless quality of her words made him want to be reckless and ditch his plan right now, to pull her out of the party and run off this very minute.

*Not yet*, he told himself. *Take your time.* "I'm close. Dad and I drew up the succession plan last week. It's got a ways to go

yet—we still don't agree on everything—
but we're working on it."

She smiled, and he began calculating how
they could make it out the door…until Pauline came around the corner.

"There you are!" she said with mock annoyance. "Chaz, honey, I'm going to have
to drag Yvonne away from you for something important."

He enjoyed how reluctantly Yvonne
slipped from his side, keeping hold of his
hand until the last possible moment.

He walked back into the reception and
stood by Dad while Pauline, Yvonne and
some other women talked in an excited knot
on the other side of the room.

"Do you get it now, son?" Dad clamped
his hand on his shoulder, his smile broader
than it had been in the church. The man
looked about to bust from happiness. When
Chaz called him two nights ago to say he
was booking a flight to the valley, he was

sure he had heard the old man choke up a bit.

Chaz returned his stepfather's smile. "As a matter of fact, I do." It felt as if his soul couldn't hold all the joy he felt today. He was here. Dad was married. Yvonne was beside him. Wander would be his. He had to keep telling himself it was real. The anger he'd leveled against God for taking everything away from him had slowly transformed into gratitude for today's even greater blessings. For the first time in far too long, his soul felt like peace and redemption were possible, gifts from God he could open his hand and accept. *Everything really does work together for good, doesn't it, Mom?*

The thought drew him to feel in his pocket for a different kind of heirloom, the happiest one he could imagine. Tell Dad now? Or wait and let him have the day's joy all to himself?

Opting for restraint, Chaz simply turned

and shook his father's hand. "You got yourself a good one, Dad."

His stepfather beamed. "I did, didn't I?" He rocked back on his heels. "Useful little pair of words, 'I do.'" Dad nudged him as if they were school buddies. "Y'oughta try 'em sometime. I mean, you've already got the hardware, right?"

Chaz tried to hide his surprise. Did Dad somehow know he had his mother's diamond ring in his pocket? The heart-shaped stone was Mom's from her first marriage to his dad, from before Hank had come into the picture. Mom had given it to him in her final days, asking him to keep it until the time he chose to give his heart. "I'll never get to meet her," she'd said with tears in her weary eyes, "but this way she'll know I'm glad for her."

*You'd love Yvonne, Mom.* The thought pinched his heart a bit, but it could sit there beside the joy and he'd be okay. *I love Yvonne.*

Suddenly, he needed Dad to know. Chaz

dipped into his pocket and sheepishly pulled out the ring to show his father. Dad responded with the biggest hug Chaz could ever remember receiving from the man.

"Now's not too soon," Hank teased.

Chaz shook his head. "Nah, I wouldn't spoil your day." Tonight, however, he would take Yvonne out to the gazebo, get down on one knee and make her his for the rest of his life if she'd have him.

"Spoil my day?" Dad said. "That'd be the *last* thing you would do. Nothing would make me happier."

"But Pauline. It's her day."

The band gave a dramatic drumroll. "Well, I think you're about to find out just how wrong you are about that."

"It's time to toss the bouquet!" Pastor Mitchell announced.

There were only about five single ladies to gather on the dance floor. The mischief in Pauline's eyes broadcast what was about to happen, and Chaz swallowed.

From what Chaz remembered, most brides turned their backs and tossed the bouquets over their heads.

Pauline Robinson—make that Pauline *Walker*—had never been, nor would ever be, most brides.

That woman sauntered up to stand right smack-dab in front of Yvonne. With a wink, she launched the bouquet the six inches between her and her niece.

Dad applauded and bumped him again. "Gate's been thrown wide open. All you have to do is walk through it."

Why not? If a man was going to start being spontaneous, Chaz could think of no better place than now.

Even as his stomach did somersaults, Chaz walked out onto the floor where Yvonne still stood holding Pauline's bouquet. Yvonne's eyes widened, her cheeks turning the most enthralling shade of pink as he opened his palm to show the ring inside.

He was pretty sure Pauline gave some

kind of whoop as he got down on one knee, but his pulse was roaring too loudly in his ears to know for sure. Chaz swallowed hard, told himself to reach for his dreams and the woman God was smart enough to send into his life, and looked up into Yvonne's eyes. "Yvonne Niles, will you…?"

He never got another word out. In a split second she was down beside him, arms wrapped around his neck, clinging to him as if the whole world would wash them away any second. "Yes, yes, yes," she whispered over and over as he kissed her.

# *Epilogue*

Yvonne set the sixth cupcake down in front of him and waited for Chaz to taste it.

He did, but shook his head. "Nope."

She scowled. "You're kidding. Surely this one. Wyatt loves it."

"Wyatt loves everything. That's half the man's problem."

She tried to keep her scowl, but he kissed it away, reveling in the way she melted in his arms. Snow fell in soft circles outside the bakery window, making it so only the outlines of the mountains could be seen. Everything sparkled, inside and out. *Thank You, Lord. I'm sorry it took me so long to come to my senses.* He'd forgotten how amazing happy could feel.

Yvonne pulled away just enough to nod down toward the cupcake with one lonesome bite taken out of it. "You're sure? Another bite, maybe?"

He opted for another kiss instead. "Face it. I don't like chocolate." He raised her left hand and kissed the ring he'd put on there two months ago. "There's no rule that says I have to before we get married."

"It's *my* rule." She adjusted the Wander Canyon Bakery apron he found so adorable on her. "You just haven't met the right chocolate. It's out there, and I'll find it."

He pointed to the fresh year's calendar on the wall behind her, the one with a Saturday circled in blue. "I am absolutely not postponing our wedding on behalf of a frosting flavor." He was going to carry her out of her room at the big house and across his threshold next week if he had to down a thousand cupcakes to do it.

Yvonne narrowed her eyes. "I used to bake for weddings, you know. Deadlines are my specialty."

"There's only one deadline on my calendar these days."

She picked up the cupcake he'd left behind, giving it an indulgent bite that planted a glob of frosting on her nose. "Oh, what's that?"

"The one that makes you Mrs. Walker. And it can't come fast enough." He kissed the frosting off her nose, even though it was chocolate. Some sacrifices were worth making.

\* \* \* \* \*

*If you enjoyed this story,*
*be sure to check out the other books*
*in the Matrimony Valley series:*

His Surprise Son
Snowbound with the Best Man

*Find these and other great reads at*
*www.LoveInspired.com*

Dear Reader,

I hope you've become as fond of Matrimony Valley as I have. The town and its residents have become like dear friends I'm reluctant to leave. I want to know I can always stop into Marvin's for ice cream and good advice, or indulge in Hailey's scrumptious waffle breakfasts at the Inn Love.

Good stories stay in our hearts long after we close the cover of the book. Keep watch, dear reader, for I have it on good authority that Wander Canyon will do the same very soon. After all, we haven't yet met all the unique creatures on the carousel, have we? I'm thinking Wyatt needs a story all his own…

As always, I love hearing from you. You can find me on Facebook, Twitter, Instagram and at alliepleiter.com. If good old-fashioned postal mail is your thing, you can reach me at PO Box 7026, Villa Park, IL 60181.

Blessings to you and yours,